Snow City

by

Laura Strickland

A Buffalo Steampunk Adventure

Cover Art by *Diana Carlile*

The Wild Rose Press, Inc.
PO Box 708
Adams Basin, NY 14410-0708
Visit us at www.thewildrosepress.com

Publishing History
First Edition, 2024
Trade Paperback ISBN 978-1-5092-5407-1
Digital ISBN 978-1-5092-5408-8

A Buffalo Steampunk Adventure
Published in the United States of America

Dedication

In memory of my dear friend, Cheryl.
You were there with me for all the firsts,
just two girls from Buffalo.
Only fitting you should be here with me for the last.

Chapter One

Buffalo, The Niagara Frontier, January, 1886

"Not again. Please, oh, please, not again."

Benjamin Ambrose stared at his reflection in the tall, oval mirror. Such an ordinary man. Nothing unusual in his stance or his attire. At twenty-five, he stood just under six feet, with nondescript medium brown hair and regular features set in a blatantly unmemorable face. He might be any random inhabitant of the city of Buffalo.

No one would ever guess by looking at him that he'd lost track of how many times he'd died. Was it twelve? Fourteen? No matter, and no time to figure that out now. For it was about to happen again.

He could tell by the tingling in his toes. They always started pricking when he was about to die, like a foot that had fallen asleep and gone numb. The numbness spread upward very slowly, giving him a precious few moments of warning.

Moments to try and prepare.

The first time it had happened to him, he'd been four years old. He didn't retain a lot of memories from so far back, but he remembered that. He'd been playing with the building set he loved, up in the hallway of this very house here on Virginia Street. When the tingling started in his toes, he'd thought he'd been kneeling too long and had shifted position. It hadn't helped and he'd got scared, abandoning his toys and running down the stairs to find his mother in the kitchen. *Trying* to run down the stairs.

The numbness had engulfed his legs halfway down, and he'd tumbled the rest of the way, making a terrible racket that had, indeed, brought his mothing hurrying.

He'd been dead when he hit the floor at the bottom.

An ambulance porter had been the one to bring him back that time. By luck or, as his mother always insisted, providence, there'd been an ambulance on the street when his father—who was still alive back then—ran out. The porter and driver had arrived in moments, and the porter, who'd had a boy Benjamin's age at home, had refused to give up on him.

Within five minutes, he'd brought Benjamin back to life.

Mother, who had watched the whole procedure with frantic attention, had attempted to do the same on subsequent occasions. She'd called to him. Laid hands on him. Massaged his chest. Slapped him.

All to no avail.

Benjamin himself never remembered being dead. He knew about this part—the onslaught, as he called it. And he recalled some if not all his returns to life. The recoveries, which varied as to time and intensity of consequences.

He had no idea what might happen if he fell down, stricken, here in the house while alone, with no one at hand to recall him. Would he remain dead? Would it all end?

He turned from the mirror where he'd been knotting his tie before beginning his day, and made for the door of his bedroom. Just outside it lay the hallway where he'd been playing with his blocks the first time this happened, some twenty-one years ago.

By the time he reached it, his thighs were numb. He grasped the frame of the door to keep himself upright and called down the stairs.

"Mother? Mother!"

Just the two of them inhabited the house since Father's illness and death six years ago. There had been no hope of saving David Ambrose. They had known for nearly a year that they were going to lose him. Now just Benjamin, his mother, and two aging automatons occupied the tall, narrow house.

"Benjamin?"

The numbness had reached his waist. When it claimed his heart, he would die.

"Benjamin!" His mother's voice came from the bottom of the stairs. He heard her come clattering up, the sound of her shoes on the oak risers, and her head came into view, wavy and brown. Her face, turned to him in horror, appeared like a moon rising. White and strained, her wide brown eyes so like his own, stricken.

"No," she cried. "No!"

"Get Mrs. McMahon," he implored, quite possibly his last words.

Their neighbor, Clara McMahon—once Clara Allen—had a talent, a peculiar one she kept very much under wraps. Benjamin imagined she did so because she did not want to be labeled a freak, and who could blame her? Did Benjamin not do the same with his affliction?

He had a propensity to perish without warning. Clara McMahon brought people back to life. Curious that they should live next door to one another, and had for years.

Her house tended to be as busy as his and Mother's

was quiet, full of children she fostered and one of her own. Her husband operated a coffin shop—also a fitting sort of irony.

Benjamin always thought how convenient it would be for Mother should he fail to return to life one of these times.

Maybe this time.

Benjamin knew about Clara McMahon's talents only because he'd availed himself of her services once before when he'd also died here at home. Not that first time but only eight or nine years ago when Father had still been alive.

The way Father had told the tale, Benjamin had collapsed and Father had run out into the street, desperate to find an ambulance, and had encountered Clara. She had followed him back in and—well, revived Ben.

He'd had strong feelings toward her for a while after that. He'd watched her house and hoped for a glimpse of her, but she'd kept strictly away from him, and since he was a quiet and retiring young man, they'd failed to encounter one another. After a year or so, the impulse to see her, to be in her company and to touch her, had worn off.

Mother gained the top of the stairs and reached out for him. The numbness rose into his chest like cold fingers grasping for his heart.

He fell onto the hall carpet and knew no more.

****

People often wondered about death. Was there an afterlife? Did one encounter deceased relatives on the way, or a tunnel of light? Did the spirit endure? Did sensation accompany the experience of passing?

Benjamin could only speak for himself. When he

died, he knew nothing at all. He heard no celestial harps, no heavenly angel voices. He was aware of nothing until he came alive again.

In this instance, the first thing he saw was Clara McMahon's face. It was a very nice face, for Clara was quite a pretty woman. She had eyes of a peculiar gray-green color now fixed intently on his as if attempting to keep hold of him. Curls of caramel brown escaped from a messy bun, graced a brow furrowed by tension, or perhaps concentration. Her hands grasped Benjamin's where he lay flat on his back upon the floor near the top of the stairs.

Behind her stood a second, larger form—her husband, Liam. Benjamin wondered dimly why Liam wasn't at work and concluded that it must be too early yet for him to have left the house.

Benjamin could hear his mother weeping—in relief, no doubt—though she remained out of his line of sight. Well, his senses were working, so he must be alive.

"Mr. Ambrose?" Clara said softly. "Are you here with us?"

She could at least call him *Benjamin*, since she would have just finished kissing him. That was how she brought people back to life, by placing her mouth on theirs and breathing her own life force into them. And that might explain why her husband, a big Irishman, glowered at him while standing poised like a great guard dog.

It might also explain why she looked so very beautiful to Benjamin. The connection formed between them still flared bright and strong.

"I'm here." His voice came in a croak. She looked relieved. Her expression eased a bit, and she let go of his hands.

Mother, on her knees also, pushed in and grasped them in turn. "Benjamin? Son?"

"Mother, it's all right."

Truly, though, it wasn't. He felt undeniably strange, his body vibrating all over as new life flowed through him. His lungs sought for air. His mind sought for far more. It wanted those blank moments back, when he'd lain dead, wanted to fill them with his perceived reality.

He said inconsequentially, "I'm going to be late to work."

Clara smiled. She glanced at Liam, who gave a shrug.

"You'd best lie there a minute or so," Liam said in his rich Irish brogue. "'Tis a strange sensation, as I know."

Rumor had it Clara had once brought her handsome husband back to life, before he became her husband, that was.

"But," Benjamin repeated doggedly, "I'll be late. For work."

Liam gave a rakish laugh. "I'm sure, my lad, your employer will understand."

"I can't tell Mr. Carter I died and came back again." Mitch Carter was one of the wealthiest men in the city, if you didn't count the collective wealth of the automatons who, now they were required by law to be paid for their services, tended to pool their money. Mr. Carter was also not a man you wanted to cross. Though he'd always been fair and decent to Benjamin, he had connections to the underbelly of this city.

"No," said Clara. "I suppose not. Liam, can you help him up?"

Liam did so. The man had a prodigious strength, which Benjamin supposed might be expected of someone who heaved coffins around all day for a living. Now he heaved Benjamin up and stood him on his feet.

Those feet trembled. Strength returned, but slowly and most reluctantly this time, so it seemed, muscle by muscle. He must truly have been gone.

Mother, with tears still running down her face, wrapped her arms around him and looked at Clara.

"How can I ever thank you?"

Clara too seemed rattled and as if she sought to put the pieces of herself back together. Benjamin wondered what it required to bring someone back to life.

"That's perfectly all right, Mrs. Ambrose."

Clara turned her gaze on Benjamin. She looked concerned. "Are you feeling quite yourself yet, Mr. Ambrose?"

He did not feel himself, not at all. But as he noticed belatedly, she'd run out of her house in her wrapper, and no doubt wanted to get home.

Foolishly, he said, "You really should call me Benjamin."

Liam growled, and Clara gave a faint smile.

Liam poked a finger at Benjamin's chest. "You're Mr. Ambrose and she's Mrs. McMahon, and don't go gettin' any ideas, right?"

"Certainly not, Mr. McMahon."

"Come. Benjamin, you had best lie down." Mother tugged him toward his bedroom. "Mrs. McMahon, if you ever require anything or need my last drop of blood—"

"That won't be necessary, Mrs. Ambrose. I'm just grateful I was at home and available."

"So am I."

"If you would do me one favor…" Clara's curiously colored eyes became troubled, "I would appreciate you not speaking of this—"

"Of course not," Mother and Benjamin both said.

One of the household automatons came rattling up the stairs. Benjamin would not like to say that curiosity had brought it, though in this case Winston no doubt came out of both curiosity and concern.

"Madam, allow me to help," the unit said. The battered face came into Benjamin's view. He blinked at it.

"Yes, Winston, please help me."

Benjamin expected Clara and Liam to leave when Mother and Winston led him away, but Clara touched Liam on the arm and followed them. Benjamin leaned on Winston heavily, moving like an old man. He always hurt dreadfully with the return of sensation to his muscles, and surely more than usual this time. He knew from experience he'd have bruises where he fell and his body, drained of vital humors when he died, might ache for days.

But however you looked at it, that beat remaining dead.

Chapter Two

"How do you feel?"

The question came not from Mother, who still sought to pull herself together, but from Winston. The unit had helped Benjamin to his bed, where he now lay atop the coverlet like a corpse in its satin-lined coffin, and continued to stare at him worriedly.

The automaton's face had once been skillfully painted. Over the years, the paint had weathered and worn away so that it now appeared more a suggestion of features than otherwise. Faded blue eyes, chipped eyebrows, nostrils long worn off. Winston had never possessed lips, just a cloth screen where his mouth should be, with a voice box installed behind it.

Benjamin had done what he could for Winston over the years. Repainted his features a few times. Paid for maintenance on all his joints. It seemed the least one could do, for one's best friend.

Not that Benjamin did not have human friends. He did. But for as long as he could remember, Winston had been there. Had played with him as a child. Had, as now, comforted him.

"I feel awful," he admitted to the unit.

"Like after a shutdown?" Winston inquired.

Benjamin smiled ruefully. "Like after a shutdown." Benjamin did his best to assure that happened as seldom as possible for Winston. But perhaps being periodically shut down for maintenance or other causes allowed Winston to sympathize with Benjamin's peculiar predicament.

For he always had.

"I should have been with you, Master Benjamin, the sooner to summon help."

"You cannot be with me at every moment."

"This is true. But—"

The automaton was interrupted when Clara stepped up. Her pretty face still looked pale and strained, her gaze understanding. "Do you think I might have a word, Mr. Ambrose? If you don't feel equal to it and prefer us to come back later, we can be on our way. I have a houseful of children wanting their breakfasts."

Benjamin looked at her in inquiry. He felt the fool lying there on his bed, fully dressed with her—and Liam at her back—looming above him. At the same time, it pained him to watch her walk away. The result of connections forged during his revival, no doubt.

"Please go ahead, say what you wish."

Her look of concern deepened. To his surprise she came and perched on the edge of his bed. "Mr. Ambrose, your predicament is a dangerous one. These episodes of yours—have they been increasing in frequency? In—in intensity?"

"No, I don't think so." It would be difficult for the experience to be more intense than *dead*.

She studied him kindly. "Nonetheless, you might want to speak with someone about this. When we were connected, when I brought you back, I sensed—"

Now, out of the morass of his confusion, Benjamin felt a spear of cold disquiet.

"Talk to someone?" He withdrew from her, much as

he still craved her touch. "You mean, like a doctor?"

He'd had enough of doctors when young. His parents had at first supposed his was a physical affliction and had taken him to every physician they could find. The quacks had strung them along, subjecting Benjamin to supposed cures and treatments, many of them harrowing. The honest ones, like the last, Mr. Crowder, had pronounced him physically well and healthy.

"There is nothing wrong with your son that I can find, Mrs. Ambrose," Crowder had said with a look of bafflement. "I would suggest you consult a psychiatrist."

They had—only one. He had subjected Benjamin, then around ten years old, to a series of electrical jolts produced by a steam plant that had chugged and clattered. He still heard that steam plant in his ill-favored dreams.

Mother had broken after she and Father brought him home from that session. She'd wept over Benjamin and cried to Father, "David, that is enough. We are not putting him through this treatment ever again."

Since that time, he'd only seen doctors for mundane matters—sore throats or the like, accidents like the time his hand had been slammed in the door of a cab. And he never informed those physicians of his affliction.

Mother came pressing in now, all her defenses raised. "Absolutely not, Mrs. McMahon. If you know how he's been treated in the past—we must keep this a secret."

Clara's compassion merely deepened. "I understand. But—"

"If they decide he's mad," Mother lowered her voice to a frantic whisper," they'll drag him away to that place on Forest Avenue. Lock him up for life."

The place on Forest Avenue was the fancy new psychiatric hospital Mr. Richardson had designed. State of the art it was said to be. A state of the art prison for crazy men.

Ben sat up in the bed. Surely he could speak for himself. "Mother—"

"Benjamin, I will protect you in any way I can."

"Mrs. Ambrose." Clara did not move from her place on the edge of the mattress. "It is not a matter of protecting your son." She glanced again at Liam, who still hovered at her shoulder. "Each time he is brought back from death, I suspect it takes a toll."

Liam grunted acknowledgement. To Benjamin he said, "I can't imagine how you've withstood it more than once, old son. You must have a constitution like an ox."

"I'm strong."

Clara laid her fingers on his and comfort flowed through him. "I have no doubt you are. But when I brought you back this time I could feel—feel you did not come back all the way. I fear," her warm gaze moved to Mother, "I fear there may come a time when no one and nothing will be able to bring him back."

Releasing Benjamin's hand, she rose and staggered slightly. Restoring Ben had indeed taken much from her. Liam's hands were there in an instant, lending support.

"Come, my love. Enough."

She leaned into him, but her gaze returned to Benjamin. "I fear these episodes of yours may have a spiritual cause. No, not mental—" She flicked a glance at Mother. "But, Mr. Ambrose, when I connected with you I could feel a disturbance in your spiritual body. You have a—" she sought visibly for words, "a very deep and perhaps very ancient spirit."

Ancient? Whatever did she mean by that? He was only twenty-five.

Clara leaned more heavily into Liam. "Mr. Ambrose, have you ever heard of Mrs. Topaz Gideon? She used to be Topaz Hathor."

Benjamin nodded. Most of the city had heard of her. But it was Mother who answered. "Isn't she the woman who's working with the—er—prostitutes? To improve their lots?"

"She is so much more than that. She is also a gifted spiritual medium and advisor. She might be able to help you."

Mother immediately recoiled. "Oh, I don't think—"

But Clara's gray-green gaze remained fixed unblinking on Benjamin's. "Mr. Ambrose?"

All at once he felt exhausted. He blinked at her. "You think the cause of me dying is—is deep within me. In my spirit."

She nodded solemnly.

"How could this Mrs. Gideon help me?"

"I am not sure she can. But she has the ability to see into the spiritual world. And she knows others who possess similar abilities. If she cannot help you, she may know someone who can."

"How best might I contact her?"

"She has a home for reclaimed women over on Ellicott Street. The Haven for Disadvantaged Women, she calls it. You might best connect with her there. Mention to her that I suggested you get in touch."

Ben had no intention of doing so. In fact he could not even imagine taking such a step. Yet at the moment his connection with Clara remained intense and he wanted to please her. So he nodded.

"Come, my love." Liam tugged at her arm. "Away home."

"Clara's gaze clung to Ben's as Liam led her from the room. "Please think about what I said, Mr. Ambrose."

"I will."

They went out of the room and clattered down the stairs. Mother accompanied them, still talking. Ben and Winston were left staring at one another.

Ben now ached from head to foot as if someone had beaten every inch of him with a stick, and his heart thumped in his chest rather like that steam plant he remembered from the psychiatrist's treatment room when a child.

Was it true what Clara had said? Did he lose a little bit of himself every time he died and came back again?

If so, why? And would the day come when the balance tipped so he couldn't be brought back and he slid away into what Clara called the spiritual realm?

The prospect completely unsettled him. Despite the somewhat dull parameters of his life—dull except for the intervals during which he died—he liked being in the world. He enjoyed his job working for Mitch Carter, helping select the orphanages that magnate of the city purchased and revamped. Even though his life felt rather empty and hollow at times.

Hollow. Was that what Clara meant? Was he becoming hollowed out by the repeated loss of life?

He squeezed his eyes shut and groped within. All the pieces of him still seemed to be there. The memories. The preferences and the quirks. The voice that talked in his head, the one that made him *him*.

And something else. A vibration, a kind of energy that felt as if it flowed through the threads of his being.

A current connected to—

What? Nothing specific that he could tell. Had he always harbored this?

Yes. Perhaps. Maybe not so strongly. Anyway, that stream of energy wasn't a loss, was it? That could not be what Clara meant.

He opened his eyes again.

"Here, Winston, help me up."

"Master Benjamin, do you think you should rise quite so soon?"

"I have to get to work."

"I do not think that is wise."

"I'm due to perform a tour of another orphanage on Mr. Carter's behalf this morning." And Mitch Carter wasn't the kind of man one let down.

Reluctantly, Winston helped him sit up on the side of the bed and held him there while his head spun.

When the room remained still and the furniture fell back into place, he saw Winston's face hanging close.

"I do not think, Master Benjamin, you can go to work today."

"Nonsense. It's just a matter of will."

"It's a matter of steamcabs and trolleys being shut down. I'm afraid it's snowing again outside."

Oh. Well, that was a different matter. In Buffalo, snow had the final say on everything.

Chapter Three

Snow fell thickly from a leaden sky and colored all the city white. The snow could be friendly at times. It might float down gently, making lacy patterns on railings and windows. It could coat the bare branches of trees and hedges in fluffy splendor.

This snow, reflected Magenta Rask as she struggled down Ellicott Street, was not the friendly kind. They'd not experienced that sort of gentle, decorative snow all winter. The season had begun in November when no less than ten inches had been dumped upon the city, from beneath which its citizens had dug their way out, their moods turning glum.

People who lived in Buffalo knew how to deal with winter and with snow. But a winter that began so harshly and so early did not bode well, and they knew that also.

This winter had so far lived up to its reputation. Storm upon storm had moved through, blowing up over Lake Erie, which served as an endless source of moisture, driven by fierce winds.

Now, in January, the lake had frozen over. People talking as they waited for trolleys or in the shops assured one another things would be much better when the snow machine turned off.

It hadn't been better, though, not so far. Take today. Barely eight o'clock in the morning and already half a foot had fallen. And yesterday, a good eight inches.

People shoveled, but they were running out of places to put the snow.

Magenta hastened up the street, across the sections of sidewalk that nobody had yet cleared, while the wind buffeted her fretfully, clawing her hair out from under her hat and sending it streaming. Walking west toward the river was often problematic. Never more than now.

She glanced behind to see if the dog still followed her, and her hair blew into her eyes. Today, her hair was a rich maroon-red. She had a habit of dying it as the mood struck and had so far experienced every color of the rainbow. Since she had a job and could afford it, she frequently dressed to match.

A fellow gypsy, as Topaz Gideon called her.

Peering through the driving snow, Magenta saw that yes, the dog still followed. A small scruffy specimen, it strained to reach above the level of the snowbanks and was forced to literally follow in Maj's footsteps, jumping from one bootprint to the next. Yet it persisted.

Pity flooded her heart and she stopped and turned around. She might wear the aspect of someone tough and uncaring, a shell she'd grown over the years after being buffeted by life much as she was now buffeted by the wind. People took her as hard, even brittle. The truth was she felt entirely too much.

Animals usually knew the truth about her, and that was why they tended to seek her company. She believed they could sense not what she displayed but what she felt.

She looked at the dog and, as best it was able, since it appeared to have but one eye, it looked back at her.

"Off with you, now," she told it. "You can't follow me."

The dog sat down, trembling, in one of her bootprints.

"Oh, hell," Magenta breathed. She couldn't possibly take the dog to the Haven, where she worked. They'd already taken in three cats and a large dog, all of which had followed Magenta there on other occasions. Topaz— her employer—would put her foot down.

The Haven was the Haven for Disadvantaged Women, operated by Mrs. Topaz Gideon, a refuge for prostitutes who wished to retire from the life.

Magenta had never worked the streets but only because she'd had other skills that she'd preferred to employ. Thievery had kept her fed at her worst moments.

She'd met Topaz several months ago by chance, she'd say, if she believed in chance. She didn't. Topaz had recognized something in her, perhaps the same way stray animals did.

She glared harder at the dog. It raised one paw from the ground as if it wanted out of the stinging cold.

Why me? Wasn't it hard enough dealing with life on her own behalf, without worrying about the rest of the world? Without, on some level, feeling what others felt?

Even the city. She'd been wanting to tell someone the energy that ran through this place the way blood ran through a human body had gone awry. There was no one to tell—no one who would not just deem her insane.

Like people, though, places had a life force. Buffalo was a city in flux and at present not doing particularly well with it.

There were all the changes, the dark underbelly that too few souls wanted to acknowledge. There were the automatons struggling for their rights—fighting to matter, as Maj supposed everyone did, from the lowest to the highest. Last summer there'd been a sickness that had brought the whole city to its knees. It had been rooted in pure, ugly evil. And had been cured by charity.

Maj was not sure she understood it all, but for certain she could feel it all. Which was why she supposed she'd ended up working with Topaz Gideon.

Everyone ended up where she, or he, was supposed to be. In the end, that was true.

"Oh, very well," she told the dog and bent down to pick it up. About eight inches high and covered with tangled brown fur, it didn't weigh above fifteen pounds. Through the fur, its bones felt like sharp sticks.

It snuggled into Maj's arms and hid its head in her elbow. The pity that filled her promptly cracked open the door of her heart. Turning, she walked faster. The center lay just ahead. Warmth, bustle, a collection of ragged souls.

Someone—one of the automatons, no doubt—had shoveled the sidewalks and the steps leading up. Topaz employed a number of reclaimed units, aged steamies that would otherwise be sent for scrap. Maj's employer was part of a movement to refurbish them and keep that from happening. Many were rebuilt at Pike's Steam Repair Shop, and Lionel Pike was a regular visitor.

Maj let herself in the front door of the big building, out of the wind-driven snow, and sought to gather herself. Warmth struck at her, along with the combined emotions of everyone in the building. She always needed to do this—take a moment and seek to balance herself, find her center. If she didn't, she sometimes thought she would lose herself entirely among others' emotions.

Here in this building, a beloved place that had come to mean a great deal to her, she sensed so much. Hope and despair. Fear and fledgling confidence. Peril and security.

Ten women lived here, fresh off the streets. They stayed at the Haven for a time while they reacclimated—that was what Topaz called it. Then they graduated to jobs, other than those they'd had on the streets, and rooms of their own out in the world.

Maj wondered if Topaz weren't reforming her too, though she hadn't actually come out and said so.

The girls were just coming down to breakfast, filing into the big dining room that lay to the left of the entryway. A few nodded or smiled at Maj as they went past, all knowing her, some still shut down, some brittle. She stood there, trying to find her level, and heard a familiar step on the hardwood floor.

Topaz emerged from her office across the way, her boots making a staccato rhythm.

Topaz Gideon always made an entrance. She'd been Topaz Hathor once, daughter of the infamous psychic medium, Frederick Hathor, before he'd been brought down for his nefarious activities.

The descendant of gypsies, Topaz would better be dubbed the queen of them. She moved like royalty and dressed with colorful splendor. Today she wore a burgundy-colored gown heavy with elaborate embroidery, topped by a jacket of gold lamé that nearly stole Maj's breath away. The gold of the jacket closely matched Topaz's amber-colored eyes.

Topaz was not a small woman and she overtopped Maj by a good bit as she paused outside the dining room and eyed her.

"No," she said. "Oh, no. I said no more."

The dog, thus spied, did not stir. Maj could feel his

fear. And his hope.

"He followed me," she said helplessly.

"They all follow you. But just like the girls, when we have no room, we have no room. You'll have to turn him away."

Maj snorted. Topaz might talk tough, but she almost never turned girls away. They'd show up here in the middle of the night, cut or beaten. Even if it was a cot in a hallway, they always found a bed.

"It's snowing, Topaz."

"It usually is snowing."

"He only has one eye." Maj coaxed the dog's head out from the crook of her elbow and into the light. She watched the expression in Topaz's eyes change, the hard light winking out.

Topaz swore heartily.

"Just let me get him warm and dry. Feed him something."

"All right. But then he'll have to go to Jamie Kilter."

Jamie Kilter ran the Buffalo Animal Sanctuary and was heavily involved with the Anti-Cruelty League. Maj had dealt with him plenty of times and found him to be a good and compassionate man, notwithstanding the scars that disfigured half his face.

And that was the thing about Buffalo. It might be ailing in spirit at the moment, some dark energy conflicting with the brightness that should run through it. But then you had people like Jamie Kilter, working for animals. Like Topaz working for the street girls. Those who saved the broken-down automatons and fought for their rights. Those trying to revamp the orphanages. So many people working for good.

Could it overbalance the darkness? And did she,

Magenta Rask, have a place in it?

"Don't just stand there," Topaz barked. "You are dripping all over the floor."

"Sorry."

"Someone will have to mop that up."

"That'll be me."

"Damned weather. Take him to the kitchen and feed him." Topaz headed for the dining room. "Whatever you do, don't name him. And don't let the girls name him either." Her eyes flashed. "It's fatal."

Chapter Four

It sometimes took Benjamin days to recover from a bout of being dead. The lingering effects tended to hang on. The deep ache in the limbs. A general feeling of malaise and disorientation. A sense of having to grope his way back into his ordinary life.

In this instance he seemed to recover even more slowly than usual. Was that because of what Clara had told him? That his repeated experiences with death had stolen something from him? Did it stem from his own sense of being hollow? Was it merely the power of suggestion or was he fading from life?

His thoughts focused much upon Clara, but that was normal. She had breathed life back into him from the force magically available to her. That made him crave her company, long to be near her, drawn by the last remnants of that connection.

He did not, however, wish to fall afoul of Liam and perhaps die all over again.

Liam, though for the most part an amiable sort of man, wore a certain air of danger. Given he dealt with the dead and ran a coffin shop, he would doubtless have no difficulty hiding Ben's body.

In light of all that, the fact that the trolleys weren't running, and above Mother's protests—which had been vociferous—he decided to report for work.

His employer did not like excuses. All business, was

Mitch Carter. He was a hard man, the last you might expect to take on the job of overhauling the city's orphanages, except he was rumored to have been raised in one of the worst.

Ben wasn't about to go bleating to Mitch Carter about having to take a day off from work because he didn't feel himself. And Ben certainly couldn't tell him the truth. He doubted anyway that Mitch Carter would consider being dead a good enough excuse for failing to show up.

Carter's office lay situated in his home on Prospect Avenue. A fine brick house it was, with the office accessed through the rear.

The walkways had all been cleared, and the new steam car Mr. Carter had recently bought stood out front. The steam car was a thing of beauty with sculpted sides and a smooth finish, now covered by a thin layer of snowflakes.

Ben wondered that even snowflakes would dare mar such beauty.

He passed two of Mitch's men—his mind wanted to supply the word *toughs*—on his way in, and they nodded at him. Most of Mitch's men had been part of his gang when they were young and like him were products of the orphanages. The loyalty among them was darn near visible.

Ben went into the warm house gratefully, shed his outer coat, which he hung on a peg in the hallway, and tapped on Mitch's office door.

"Come on in."

Mitch sat at his desk, already at work. He shot a look at Ben, and from around the desk came the little mechanical dog, Valerie, that belonged to his wife, Tessa.

The unit spent more time with Mitch than it did with his wife.

The dog gave a single, shrill bark in greeting. Ben bent down and scratched its smooth side.

"Morning," he murmured to the dog, to Mitch, or both.

Mitch gave him a second look from narrowed, hazel eyes. "What the hell's the matter with you?"

Did it show? "Uh—not feeling quite myself this morning, Mitch."

The expression in Mitch's eyes sharpened. "Not sick, are you? If you are, get out of here."

Ever since last summer when a plague had gripped the city, Mitch had been fanatical about people bringing sickness into the house. His wife, Tessa, had been one of those stricken. Mitch, convinced he would lose her, had nearly gone mad with worry.

Ben hadn't been working for him long at that time, having been hired the previous May. Mitch had advertised for a "respectable-looking young man" to represent him in business matters, and the like. Ben found it interesting he hadn't specified he wanted a respectable man, just one who looked respectable.

"All my current employees look like criminals," he'd told Ben during the interview. It was true even of Mitch himself, though in a subtle way that defied his fine grooming and expensive suits.

Mitch treated his wife like a queen, and even before she'd fallen sick, he'd nearly shut the place down. Ben had been out of work for weeks. Tessa had fallen ill anyway. But she'd been one of the lucky ones who'd recovered.

"I'm not sick, Mitch. I just—" Ben didn't know

what to say. If his condition was worsening, would it be better to tell Mr. Carter the truth? If a bout befell him here— He didn't want his employer thinking him weak, though. "I seem to have taken a funny turn after I got up this morning. What's on the schedule for today?"

Mitch grunted and drew a laboriously written list toward him. "Three orphanage visits. I swear I never knew there were so many of the damn places in the city before I started refurbishing them."

"Excuse me." A soft voice behind Ben had him stepping aside. Tessa Carter leaned in the doorway to speak to her husband.

A lovely woman was Mrs. Carter, with a cloud of auburn hair, now piled mostly atop her head, and a fragile, delicate air. At the moment she gave off a light perfume like a whiff of apple blossoms.

Mitch's whole demeanor changed. He seemed to soften where he sat, and warmth kindled in his eyes.

"Tess?"

"I wanted to let you know I won't be going out today. I had that meeting at the women's society, but the weather's so vile it's been cancelled. I'll be staying in."

"Vile weather?" Mitch glanced at Ben, who nodded. "Again?"

"Yes, sir. It's snowing at the moment, and the wind's enough to tear your head off."

"It's always snowing lately," Mitch complained. "It makes getting around the city nearly impossible."

"Yes, sir. I saw two horse-drawn carriages stuck on Delaware Avenue when I was coming in, and a steamcab on its side. Seems the best way to get around is on foot, and that's not a treat."

Mitch looked at his wife, who had bent and picked

26

up the mechanical dog. "Good decision to stay in."

She smiled at him. "Any chance you could suspend operations for the day and stay in with me?"

Mitch flicked another look at Ben, who tried to pretend he wasn't paying attention. "It sounds like Old Man Winter may have suspended operations for me. Ben, go home."

"Eh?" He'd just got here.

"I don't think those orphanage visits will be possible today. Maybe tomorrow." Mitch's mouth quirked. "Sorry for bringing you in through the snow." He switched his gaze back to Tessa. "What's it supposed to be like tomorrow?"

She shrugged. "The weather pundits just keep calling for snow. And they predict there's what they're calling a blizzard in the offing." She made a face. "Worse than anything we've seen so far."

Mitch rubbed at his forehead. "Just what this city needs—something to make it grind to a standstill. As if there aren't already enough complications. There's supposed to be another hockey tournament. Players are already flooding in for it."

Ben groaned under his breath. The last time there'd been a hockey tournament between the Buffalo Boilermakers and the Fort Erie Freighters, it had caused a near riot. Folks here took their hockey seriously.

"Will it be cancelled?" he asked.

"Who knows? Ben, go on home. If the weather's better tomorrow, we'll reschedule the visits to the orphanages for then."

Ben nodded and went out, collecting the coat he'd just shed on the way. As he left Mitch's office, he saw Tessa circle the big desk to perch on Mitch's knee.

He experienced a sharp pang of what could only be envy. He supposed it was easy to keep a beautiful woman when you could buy her anything, though he had to admit Tessa's feelings for Mitch seemed more than genuine.

And there was Clara and Liam, who had no monetary wealth but rather seemed bound to one another on a spiritual level. No hope of anything like that for him either. He was far too ordinary—in appearance, in status, in wealth. Hell, he didn't even understand what motivated a woman to tie herself to a man. The only thing remarkable about him was his tendency to die periodically, and that certainly wouldn't attract a wife. Quite the contrary. It would be enough to frighten off any right-minded woman.

What to do now? He found himself at loose ends. He thrust his hands deep into the pockets of his coat and thought about it. He could go home and recover from this morning's shattering experience. Mother would approve. Could he tolerate a full day of her fussing over him, however? No.

Still, he retraced his steps, not sure what else to do besides head home. On the corner, a phalanx of policemen was trying to free one of the carriages, which was stuck up to its wheel hubs in a drift. Several passersby had joined in the effort that looked likely to turn the carriage over.

Ben went forward to help.

The cab driver comforted the distressed horse, which was still harnessed to the traces. A huddle of people who must have been passengers stood to one side. Ben set his shoulder between two blue-clad police officers and pushed for all he was worth.

This had become a common occurrence lately around the city. Vehicles of all descriptions got stuck on a regular basis, especially on the streets that were less traveled and thence not beaten down, or as in this case, when they got too far to one side or the other. Frequently, as now, the trams stopped running altogether.

In this case, the footing proved treacherous. As soon as Ben tried to push, he slid instead. So did the carriage.

After several seconds' effort, the police officer on Ben's left raised his head. He was a big man with bright green eyes and, as was proved when he called out, a rich Irish accent.

"We'll have to lift her, lads. She won't come out this way. Ready, now? Lift!"

Lift a carriage? Madness. But Ben found himself hooking his fingers beneath the body of the conveyance.

"Lift!" the police officer cried again, and the carriage came up out of the snow. As one, the rescuers staggered sideways and deposited it upon the beaten ruts farther over.

A ragged cheer went up. The passengers climbed back in.

"Thank you, *sor*." The police officer turned to Ben. "We can always count on the assistance of the public in a pinch. Right, Terry?"

The policeman on Ben's other side gave a grin and Ben did a double take. Something about that smile—and about the feel of these two men… Oh, but they weren't men. They were hybrid automatons. Members, no doubt, of the famed Irish Squad.

The Squad had become an institution in the city, beloved by some and detested by those who claimed automatons—and hybrids in particular, who wore skin harvested from cadavers over steel frames—were the work of the devil. Now they owned property, built churches, and even created hybrid children in their own likeness.

Ben had nothing against them. Then again, he had limited acquaintance. But he'd seen the policeman with the bright green eyes before. "You're Pat Kelly."

"Aye, *sor*, so I am." Kelly cocked his head, a purely mechanical movement. "Have we met?"

"Not officially. But everyone knows you." Pat Kelly had achieved a level of notoriety, if not fame, in this city. He seemed to be everywhere about town and could be considered the face of the struggle for automatons' rights. People liked him, or at least respected him, even his opponents, those die-hard humanists who insisted automatons had no place at all in decision making. Ben could understand why. Kelly gave off an air of trustworthiness the way a typical steamie gave off heat.

Ben wondered whether the automatons of the city would have achieved the rights they had so far without the hybrids at their head. Nearly indistinguishable from humans, they were able to speak out in the human arena and make the mechanicals' desires known. People, most people, felt comfortable with them apart from the fact that they were stronger, faster, and some said smarter than humans.

Ben stuck out his hand. "Pleased to meet you. Benjamin Ambrose. I work for Mitch Carter."

"Ah. I thought I had seen you before, *sor*. It will have been at some of the meetings concerning the orphanages."

"Yes, no doubt."

"'Tis a pleasure. Are you about Mr. Carter's

business today?"

"No, he's cancelled today's inspections because of the weather and sent me home."

"The weather is dreadful, *sor*. In all my days here, I've not seen the equal."

"Nor I. We usually have one or two bad storms per year. Not a steady stream of them."

"Would ye like an escort home, *sor*?"

"No, that's all right. I don't know whether I'm going straight home." Ben hesitated before asking on impulse, "Do you know a woman called Topaz Gideon?"

The automaton's face seemed to brighten. "Miss Topaz, *sor*? Aye indeed. She is a good friend to the ladies of the night in this city."

"So I hear."

"And daughter to the late famed spiritualist, Frederick Hathor."

"Of course." Frederick Hathor had caused a scandal when he'd died a couple of years back, in a terrible fire at his grand home.

"This center she runs for the ladies, do you know where it is?"

"On Elicott Street, *sor*."

"I need to get there, to consult her about something."

"Say no more. It's not far from here and we'll escort you. Get you through the snow a treat."

"Oh, you don't have to do that."

"One good turn deserves another. Just let us sort out this steamcab first."

Ben helped lift the steamcab off its side, just so he could say he had been a part of such a feat.

Not bad for a man who'd so recently been dead.

Chapter Five

Magenta had to give the dog a bath, because everyone at the center who encountered him complained about the smell. One or two also asked, "What is that?" which Maj considered particularly harsh.

He was quite obviously a dog and a male, as he clearly demonstrated when he tried to lift his leg on the woodwork of a doorway.

"No!" Maj hollered and he looked so chagrined she wished she hadn't been quite so loud about it.

"What's his name?" asked Lolly, one of the girls who'd been here the longest. The goal of the Haven was to get the girls off the streets if they wanted, give them a safe place to stay, let them acclimate and pursue training. Ultimately, they were meant to find jobs and places of their own.

Lolly hadn't been able to find proper work. She was, so Maj thought, just a little bit simple for someone of her years and experience.

She followed Maj into the first-floor lavatory where an offended woman, already occupying the room, cried, "Hey, you can't bring that thing in here!"

Maj told her, "You just go about your business." The woman swept out, searing Maj with her ire as she went.

It wasn't easy being able to feel others' emotions. Topaz called it a talent, but Maj would trade it away in a second if she could. She had no interest in living the life of a spiritualist.

"It's come down in the blood to you," Topaz had insisted on more than one occasion. In fact she'd mentioned it when first Maj came to her, half wild and shattered from witnessing a murder. No, from *experiencing* it. "You're quite likely part gypsy, like me."

Magenta had few guesses as to what she was, besides a thief, a survivor, and the product of the streets. She sometimes thought she could feel the streets as she walked them, feel the city and what lay beneath it.

Granite. Water. Magic.

This little creature that now trembled in her hands was part of that magic.

Lolly followed them into the lavatory.

"You going to wash him? He don't half stink."

"Yeah. You stand there, Lol, and guard the door. Don't let anybody in."

A big iron tub stood in the corner of the room, but the dog was small enough to fit in the cavernous sink, which Maj decided would be much easier.

Topaz provided soap and even lotion for the residents, the first touch of luxury some of them had ever known. Maj would just borrow some of the soap, which smelled of lavender, to improve the dog's condition.

"He's the scruffiest one you've brought in yet," Lolly observed. "Only got the one eye. What do you think happened to the other one?"

"I hate to imagine."

"I used to see strays like him when I was out on the streets. Some of those pups got treated even worse than we girls did."

Maj said nothing. She could feel the dog's emotions and Lolly's also. Darned near overwhelming.

33

"Maybe you should call him Scruffy."

"Miss Topaz says I'm not allowed to name him and he ain't staying, so don't get attached."

Lolly wrinkled her nose. "I won't."

There were already those three cats Maj had brought in and the large dog, named Fred. Topaz said the Haven being a home to the girls, there was nothing wrong with a few pets. A few.

Balancing the dog against her shoulder, Maj filled the sink with warm water and slowly lowered him in. He yipped and struggled to get back out.

"All right, it's all right. For your own good."

"Careful he don't bite," Lolly warned.

Maj soothed the animal with her hands and with her will. She ran her fingers through the tattered fur and a powerful stink arose. A cloud of brown spread through the water.

"Goodness, you are in a bad way, aren't you? No matter, we'll fix you up. Find you a proper home."

Lolly, who now leaned against the door, said, "I like the way you talk to him."

The dog liked it too and had begun to calm down. Maj worked lavender soap into his fur and began to sing to him under her breath, one of her tunes.

She didn't know where she got her tunes; they just seemed to come to her. This one made the dog relax further. In fact, all three of them had started to relax before someone tried to enter the lavatory.

Lolly threw her weight against the door. "You can't come in."

The door opened enough for one of the girls to peer through the gap. When she saw Maj and the dog, she swore volubly and went away again.

One thing that could be said of the women here, they had colorful vocabularies.

Magenta pulled the plug on the sink and refilled it with clean water to rinse the small dog's fur. She gently smoothed the ragged tufts back from his single eye, which proved to be brown, perfectly round, and eloquent.

"There now," she crooned again. "You're quite handsome, aren't you?"

"Let me see," cried Lolly whose heart, or so Maj suspected, was as soft as her own.

Maj drained the bowl again and dried the dog off with tender care, using one of Topaz's best towels.

"What you gonna do with that pup now, Maj?"

"Feed him, I expect. After that, if I can't find him a home, I guess he'll have to go to the animal shelter."

"That's sad." The dog had cuddled into Maj's arms. "He likes you. Wants to stay with you, I'll bet."

"The shelter's better, as you pointed out, than a life on the streets." Maj fixed Lolly with a fierce eye. "You and I both know what that's like."

No, Maj had never been forced to trade her body to men for money. In fact, she felt quite fastidious about it. But she would never condemn those who had no choice.

Heartfelt, Lolly agreed. "Anything's better than that."

****

Maj didn't admit the caller, but she heard the bell peal before someone else let him in. There was always interest when a man came to the Haven, and the girls all tended to gather in order to get a look at him, the way wasps came to a pot of sugar.

Not that many of these women equated men with

sugar. Many detested the breed. Some feared them. Most, though, just had to get a look.

Maj was more concerned with the dog, who insisted on following her everywhere. He wanted to be up in her arms except when he was eating. But she had things to do.

Topaz gave her jobs. She was adept at making lists, for one of the first things Topaz had done was teach her to read, and she was good at organizing things. They had offers of jobs come in, jobs for the girls, from all over the city. Maj was remarkably skilled at matching those opportunities up with the right women. She could just sense the fit.

There was a definite stir when the fellow came in. Maj wondered if that meant he was good-looking. There was always a considerable fuss when Topaz's husband, Romney, came calling. Now, there was a handsome man, and no mistake. Well-mannered and sophisticated, with an English accent that tended to make Maj go weak in the knees.

But a blind woman could see he belonged to Topaz and would never be anyone else's.

And that police captain, Brendan Fagan—he'd been here once or twice on official business, and was enough to make even Magenta smack her lips. A strapping fellow with eyes blue enough to be seen across a room, and a warm Irish brogue besides.

Every time he showed up, the women fair went mad to steal a look, even though, just like Maj, they should abhor policemen.

Maybe it was that accent, again. Though if Maj had a man of her own—and she certainly didn't anticipate that ever happening—he'd have to be of the city, one hundred percent.

The desk where she worked was situated in a corner of what was called the work room, where the girls trained, studied, and practiced many a trade. While she sat there with her lists and the dog on her feet, two of them—Gracey and Della—came in.

"Ordinary, I'd call him," declared Della. "Nothing special to look at."

"A gentleman, though," said Gracey, "from what I could see. Dressed in a proper suit of clothes. And a paddy wagon dropped him off."

"A paddy wagon?" That caught Maj's attention.

"Yeah. One drawn not by horses but hybrid policemen."

"Well, well. You don't say."

"Quite the sight."

"Do you think the visitor's a hybrid?"

"Didn't look like one."

Well, but sometimes it was hard to tell except—well, folks give off different vibrations, don't they? Just like the various areas of the city did. If she got close enough to pick up on that—

But there was no way she was getting that close to strange gentlemen callers.

Chapter Six

To say Ben found Topaz Gideon striking would be an understatement of epic proportions. The first word that sprang to mind upon beholding her was *intimidating*, closely followed by a second: *beautiful*.

In fact most everything about this day so far had been intimidating, including that harrowing ride he'd just endured inside the paddy wagon through streets clogged with snow. He'd never experienced anything like it. If it did not stop snowing soon, the city would self-destruct.

And now—Topaz Gideon.

She stood nearly as tall as he did, and him almost six feet. Of course she did wear a pair of quite remarkable boots with stacked heels, the uppers made of embossed leather. She also wore—well, Benjamin supposed it would be called a lady's suit, of deep scarlet. The jacket, made of ruffled gold silk, hung open over an equally ruffled blouse and displayed Mrs. Gideon's more than ample curves. Nothing about her was petite.

She led him into her office, turned, and met his gaze with a pair of tawny golden eyes that contrasted starkly with her black hair.

"Ah, Ambrose, what can I do for you?"

Ben hesitated, not sure how to frame his request.

Her cool, rather uncanny gaze studied him. "I hope you have not come here under the misapprehension that you might hire a female companion."

"Uh—no. It's not that."

"Good, because contrary to what some gentlemen seem to believe, this is a place where our ladies come for sanctuary and to begin anew."

"Very admirable. No, it's you I wanted to see." That sounded terrible, and he flushed with mortification. "It's a—a spiritual matter."

Her gaze cooled farther. "I do not do that work anymore."

"I see. I'm very sorry I troubled you, then. It's just that I'm at my wits' end, and my neighbor, Clara McMahon, suggested—" He began to turn away, hat in hand.

Topaz Gideon drew a breath. "Wait."

He looked back at her. She had drawn herself up and stood stiffly. As he watched, she inhaled again, deeply as if scenting the air and closed her eyes. He could feel her thinking. Reaching.

When her eyes opened once more, they looked so bright it startled him.

"Mr. Ambrose, you have recently been dead."

"Yes," he said miserably.

Her eyes widened. "This has happened to you more than once."

"Yes. It keeps happening to me."

"Perhaps you had better sit down."

****

Ben perched on the plain wooden chair facing the desk behind which Topaz Gideon sat. She didn't interrupt while he struggled to explain his situation. Instead she listened quietly and with great attention.

He thought he did a poor job, though, of relating his

somewhat complicated history. He'd never told anyone all of this before, and it did not come out quite coherently.

"So," she spoke when at last he finished, "you experienced this again just this morning?"

"Yes."

"Incredible." Topaz Gideon blinked. "How are you feeling?"

"I—well, rather unsteady, if I'm honest. There's the aftermath of dying, which always leaves me feeling a bit wrung out, I guess I'd call it. And the aftermath of being brought back by Mrs. McMahon. I have feelings for her, if you understand. Oh—" He flushed. "I promised I wouldn't tell anyone what she'd done. Though she was the one who suggested I come to you."

"You may rely upon me for silence."

"And then there's the frustration and the helplessness of it all. Being stricken out of the blue with no more than a tingling to give me warning."

"Yes."

"I'm only twenty-five. I want to be able to live my life. Clara suggested I might be, well, losing a little of myself each time I come back. And that a spiritualist might be able to advise me before—before it's no longer possible to bring me back."

"And Mrs. McMahon suggested me." Topaz gave a tight smile. "I suppose I have a reputation."

"You—you do know about spiritual things, so I understand. The other realm."

"Yes." She repeated. "As I said, I don't do that work anymore, but it is not something from which one can ever separate oneself completely. I find your situation compelling. I have, during my time, encountered many spirits of the dead. But they were *dead*. Or alive and separated from their body. There's never been one who died and came back again.

"But I can also sense auras—the spirit which dwells within each of us. The living being, so to speak."

"Can you—er—sense mine?"

"Oh, yes."

Before he could ask if there was something amiss with his spirit, if it were ill or cursed, she got to her feet and walked around the desk to the door, where she asked someone to bring tea.

When she returned to the desk, she said, "You are looking a little peaky, Mr. Ambrose."

"Me? Or my spirit?"

She smiled. "Both."

"Can you—can you tell if I am cursed? It's the only real explanation I can come up with. If there's some evil spirit hanging around me—" He felt ridiculous even voicing that, but he'd already told his mad tale to this woman.

"Mr. Ambrose, there is no such thing as an evil spirit. A spirit is a force, an energy, part of a much greater source. It may act in a malevolent fashion due to past experience. But all energy is, in essence, pure."

Not certain he understood all of that, Ben shifted his hat on his knee. "Are any malevolent spirits attached to me?"

"No. I sense no dead with you." Again her lips twisted. "Except yourself."

"Oh. You can't help me, then."

"I did not say that."

A girl came in with a teapot and two cups on a tray. She gave Ben a sideways look.

"Thank you, Frannie."

Ben eyed the tray with disfavor. "Mrs. Gideon, I did not come here to drink tea."

"I don't have time for it either, but as I say, I can tell by looking at you—if not by sensing you—that you need fortification." Matter-of-factly, she poured the tea. "Drink that."

It proved to be excellent tea, full-bodied and with a fruity, exotic flavor, like Topaz herself, he thought.

Topaz drank and sat back a little. "As I say, I have encountered many spirits, but—I must tell you—never one like yours."

"Oh?" He didn't know if that was bad or good.

"It is—immensely old, I think. And has returned to this world many times."

Startled, he asked, "Do spirits do that?" Reverend Byler at the Presbyterian Church said they had only one chance at redemption.

"Oh, yes. But your spirit seems"—she tipped her head—"I do not want to say *sick*."

His stomach churned. He did not want a sick spirit which it seemed would be just a step above malevolent.

"I would rather say *disturbed*."

Well, that didn't seem much better. One step up from madness. He'd told Mother he'd end up in Mr. Richardson's psychiatric hospital. Perhaps he'd been right.

"The way water may be disturbed when a hand reaches in and stirs a basin," she elucidated. "Of course that could merely be a product of your most recent demise."

"I see," Ben lied. He didn't.

For the first time she looked sympathetic. "It must

be most distressing."

She could not imagine.

"Can you tell what is causing this disturbance?"

"No. Can you? What has been happening in your life? What occurs when you experience these episodes?"

"Nothing much. I have a quiet life." Far too quiet. "Mother and I live alone. It has been difficult to keep a job because of the—er—episodes. I work for Mitch Carter now, representing him during inspections of the orphanages he buys, facilitating the purchases and overseeing the inspections after."

"Does Mr. Carter know about—"

"No one knows. Except my neighbor. And now you."

"And, Mr. Ambrose, what do you do for recreation? For entertainment? Do you belong to a gentleman's club, for instance? Do you see a lady or gentleman?"

"Not really." Ben flushed again. "How can I get serious about a woman, if I might die in front of her?"

"You might confide your predicament."

"I couldn't possibly."

"You just have confided in me."

"She'd think me mad." A bit desperately, Ben said, "Don't you see? I must get to the bottom of this, figure out why it keeps happening to me, before it takes too much out of me. Before I die and can't come back again. Can you help me?"

"No, Mr. Ambrose."

His heart fell. His face must have reflected his emotion, for she swiftly said, "I cannot help you, but I may know someone who can."

Again she rose from the desk and went to the door where she asked someone, "Tillie, will you please call

Magenta?"

Magenta? He was pretty sure that was a color and not a person. Yet for some reason the name lodged in Ben's brain.

Topaz waited at the door until someone arrived. Another woman.

She stood nowhere near Topaz's height and carried a very small, very damp brown dog in her arms. Like Topaz, she wore colorful clothing, a skirt of bright mustard yellow and a jacket over it that looked as if it had been sewed out of a dozen different fabrics.

Her hair was—goodness, the most outlandish color. Brownish-purple-red, and there was a lot of it. She wore it caught back from a pointed, piquant face. Her eyes were so dark as to appear black.

She looked small and graceful and perfect in a way Ben couldn't explain.

"Mr. Benjamin Ambrose, meet Miss Magenta Rask."

Chapter Seven

Had the floor just shifted beneath Maj's feet? She couldn't be sure, though the dog sort of scrambled around in her arms as if he felt it too, and sought more secure purchase.

It felt as if the currents she always subliminally sensed flowing beneath the earth had gathered their forces and subtly changed direction.

That couldn't be due to this man who'd risen from his chair and turned to face her. He looked far too ordinary.

Of a good height, with nice, broad shoulders under a fine-quality coat, he looked like a typical man of the city and unlikely to rock anybody's world. He had plain brown hair, neatly cut, and a face altogether unmemorable. A broad forehead, slightly square jaw. At the moment she thought he looked pale and a little unwell.

His eyes—now, they were very nice. Brown like hot chocolate, one of her very favorite things that she'd never, ever had before coming here.

Her other senses went to work as they tended to do, whether she wanted them to or not. She could feel him, a kind of miasma of uncertainty and doubt and hopefulness and—yeah, there came the impact. It fair rocked her back on her heels.

Who was he? Benjamin Ambrose, yes. But *who*?

"Pleased to meet you," she murmured and juggled the dog to put out her hand. Given what she sensed, she both did and did not want to touch this man.

He pressed his palm to hers and inclined his head. The kickback was so strong she had to catch her breath. Didn't he feel that? Apparently not, for he looked far too calm.

"Why are you holding a wet dog?" he asked.

"He's a stray from out of the storm. They tend to follow me."

"I see."

"Don't worry, he doesn't bite."

Topaz watched them closely. Maj glanced at her. "Umm—what's this all about?"

"I believe I have found an assignment for you, Magenta."

Maj gestured behind her. "I already have my regular work."

"This would be something extra that would benefit both you and Mr. Ambrose."

No. Oh, no.

No doubt reading her accurately, Topaz went on, "It will help you develop your spiritual abilities. Mr. Ambrose, Magenta is a sensitive. A very acute one, so I estimate, but she has yet to sound the depths of her acuity, so to speak. I propose putting the two of you together for mutual benefit."

Mr. Ambrose said nothing. He stared at Maj as if she'd just popped up through the floor.

Maj said, "I don't want—" She broke off. She'd come to Topaz in considerable need and imagined Topaz would say it wasn't about what she wanted. "He's all in a tangle."

"You can feel that, can you?"

"Of course I can feel that."

"Excellent. It's a beginning. Mr. Ambrose, do you agree to work with Miss Rask?"

"I'm not sure what that would entail."

"Neither am I, quite yet. Spend time in one another's company. See what comes forth—on a spiritual level, that is."

"I have my regular work," Maj protested again.

"As do I," said Ambrose.

"Well, I suppose you'll have to meet up after hours then, on your own time."

Ambrose nodded. He reached out with a careful hand and petted the dog, which lay huddled in Maj's arms all this while. The movement brought him very close to Maj.

"What's his name?"

"He doesn't have one."

"Oh?" The chocolate brown eyes questioned her. "Why not?"

Maj shot a look at Topaz. "I'm not allowed to name him, or I'll end up keeping him."

Mr. Ambrose gave a laugh. The dog licked his hand.

"So, Miss Rask, are you willing to work with me?"

"Oh, I guess it will be all right."

****

"So what was that about?" Maj asked after Mr. Ambrose left.

Topaz shut the door of her office carefully before she answered. "You felt what's inside him." Her gaze met Maj's. "The 'tangle' as you called it."

"Yeah." She wasn't sure she wanted to dip her toe into that.

"He needs help, quite plainly. And you need to develop your talent if you're ever to do more than schedule job interviews."

Maj's chin rose. "Maybe I like scheduling job interviews. It's satisfyin'."

"So it is. But is it your destiny?"

Maj shivered. "I don't like destiny. And," she jerked her head at the door, "I'm not sure I like him."

"He seems like a nice young man."

"He *seems*, sure." Maj said darkly, "There's an awful lot there."

"Yes. He has an unfortunate propensity for dying. Perhaps you can discover just what's amiss and sort him out so he can live a peaceful life."

"Peaceful's good." A propensity for dying? Maj gathered that meant he made a kind of habit of it. Had it happened more than once? No wonder he felt the way he did.

Topaz gave a brisk nod. "When he contacts you, set up a meeting. Somewhere neutral." She made a face. "If this weather ever settles down."

"The weather." Maj waved a hand, startling the dog. "The city. Maybe even him. It might all be wound up together."

Topaz smiled. "You'll have a lot to unravel."

"I don't like unraveling. It makes me impatient."

"A good way to learn some self-discipline, then. Magenta." Topaz's gaze turned serious. "You have a gift. You can either try to deny it, or embrace it responsibly."

"Responsible? Me?"

"An ironic juxtaposition, I'll admit."

"Whatever that is."

"Look, that young man's welfare could rest in your

hands. He's troubled and miserable. You could make him less so. Just like"—Topaz gestured—"that dog."

Well. If she thought of Mr. Ambrose as a lost dog, it might not be so bad.

"All right." The weather would likely interfere with any proposed meetings anyway. She could put Benjamin Ambrose right out of her head.

Except, as it subsequently proved, she couldn't. While she went about her business for the rest of that day, he seemed to balance there right at the front of her brain. A flash of how he'd looked when she'd first seen him standing there in Topaz's office, in his long coat. A memory of those eyes of his that held so much in the way of banked emotion. A remnant of the jumbled emotions he made her feel.

It was like when she used to break into houses. She could feel the right ones to go for, and the ones to leave alone. And when she got inside—because she almost always did—she could tell where to go to find the valuables. And she could feel when there was a treasure, when she was onto something good.

Mr. Ambrose felt a little bit like that.

But if she'd learned one thing, it was that it didn't do to get involved. In and out—with people and with situations both. Don't linger, because that was when you got caught.

She'd put the little dog on the floor beside her desk when she went back to work. Now he stood up with his front paws on her knee and looked into her face with his single, earnest eye.

Maj realized that his eye was the exact same color as Mr. Ambrose's.

For some reason, she shivered. Then she lifted the

dog onto her knee and cuddled him close.

If she was going to have anything to do with Mr. Ambrose, she'd have to follow Topaz's suggestion and think of him as just another needy stray. Dogs were so much easier to deal with than men.

Chapter Eight

Ben felt worse the next morning, not unusual after a bout of being dead. It could take him days to regain his vitality. Even longer to collect the pieces of himself that seemed to scatter when an episode happened. Which only made him wonder whether Clara McMahon weren't all too right about him, if he didn't lose a little bit of himself each time, a piece that never quite returned.

He lay flat on his back in his bed that morning, staring up at the blank, white ceiling of his room and trying to decide which portion of him hurt the most. His back? His head? His heart.

The bedroom door creaked open and Winston trundled inside. His familiar, painted features interposed themselves between Ben and the ceiling as the automaton peered down.

"Master Benjamin? Are you well?"

Well didn't describe it. Absolutely not. Ben narrowed his eyes at Winston. "I may need a hand getting up."

"Master Benjamin, Mr. McMahon is downstairs."

"Eh?" Liam McMahon from next door? Immediately, Ben wanted to see Clara with a raw, ragged longing. He could not allow himself to go there. He could not. "What time is it?"

"Eight o'clock, Master Benjamin."

"Oh, hell. What does he want?"

"He did not specify, but he looks anxious."

"All right. Help me up."

He had bruises all down his body from the fall yesterday. Added to that, a persistent weakness dogged him.

Dog. Small, brown, scruffy. Magenta Rask.

The memory of her hit him like the proverbial ton of bricks. What kind of woman had hair that color? Couldn't be natural. And her eyes, her eyes were a bit— well, frightening.

Did he want to get mixed up with someone like that? He'd agreed to see her, but maybe he'd be better off just keeping away.

"Where is McMahon?" he asked after Winston got him up and dressed.

"Waiting in the parlor. Your mother is not yet up."

The parlor, a narrow, high-ceilinged room, felt chilly at this hour. That was probably because, as Ben saw when he glanced out the windows, it was snowing. Hard. Still. *Again.*

Liam leaped to his feet when Ben came in.

"Sorry to bother you so early, Ambrose. How are you feeling after yesterday?"

Ben smiled. "Like I got hit by a beer wagon and dragged half a mile or so."

"I hear you. Been there meself, you know."

Ben knew there was something mysterious between Liam and Clara, but he'd never heard the whole story. He'd like to, someday.

"Is something wrong, McMahon?"

"Not as such, but I wondered, old son, if I could ask a favor. I'm in a bit of a bind."

Your wife just brought me back to life. Is there

anything I can't do in return?

"What do you need?"

"You know my shop."

"Yes, of course." McMahon's Coffin Shop over on Niagara Street was flourishing, so far as Ben knew. Craftsmen, they were, and turned out a fine product.

"We're a small shop but I've been trying to expand. I've got three workers besides meself, and I recently got two of those reclaimed automatons Lionel Pike's been turning out, to help with the dogsbody work like toting bodies and sweeping up. That means I can train Reynold—Reynold Michaels—to do some assembly."

"That's good."

"Aye, it is. Only expanding costs money. I've a chance of an investor, and he's coming to see the shop today."

"Also good."

"He's a wealthy man and a quirky sort of one. Maybe you've heard of him—Bruce Buchanan?"

"Isn't he the fellow who was involved with the automaton gladiator tournament last year?"

"The very same, and he's backing the Buffalo team in next week's hockey tourney as well. You know, there's a round-robin thing going on. Players are already streamin' into the city. I met Buchanan down at Pike's shop, actually. He has more money than he knows what to do with and has decided to invest it in small businesses."

"Sorry, I don't see a problem."

"He's coming to view the shop today. And me— well, look at me. I'm rough around the edges, a workman to the bone. I'm afraid I won't represent the place well."

"Sure you will."

Liam shook his head. "Clara might stuff me in a suit, but I'll never make a gentleman. I thought you might be willing to come, just for today's meeting, and represent me."

"Me? You can talk rings around me, Liam."

"But you look the part, don't you? You're used to goin' into the orphanages and doing business for Mitch Carter, of all people."

"Yes."

"I wouldn't ask, but this is important. For my family. I want to expand the services we offer down at McMahon's. We already go and collect the dead, see, as well as make the caskets. I want to offer burials also. Maybe organize the gathering and the wake. Offer a place for folks who don't want to hold the viewing at home. But it will take a considerable influx of money."

"I still think you could represent yourself, but I'll show Mr. Buchanan around for you, if you like. What time's the meeting?"

"One o'clock this afternoon."

"I'll ask Mr. Carter if I can take my lunch late. Be at your shop then."

Relief flooded Liam's blue eyes. "Thank you, old son. I'll leave ye now. Sorry to disturb ye so early."

"Don't mention it."

Liam turned for the door where Winston stood waiting quietly to show him out. "I'll be that happy and relieved when the meeting's over as the weather permits. Did ye hear?" Liam looked back over his shoulder. "They're callin' for a blizzard next week."

"A blizzard?" Ben shot a startled glance out the door, past Winston where a new layer of snow covered the sidewalk. "What have we been having so far?"

"Damned if I know. But there's something buildin', right enough. You can feel it in the air, can't you?"

Oh yes, he could.

****

It had stopped snowing by one o'clock. A dim and watery sun appeared amid the gray clouds that streamed in from across the lake, like the belly of an enormous steamship.

As Ben had gone about his morning, visiting two orphanages and taking down information and the findings of his inspections, he'd heard nothing but talk of the weather. How much snow there'd been already. How bitter the temperatures had been. How difficult it was keeping buildings warm against the vicious wind.

A couple of people, including a woman who ran one of the orphanages, mentioned the promised—or rather threatened—blizzard. Everyone seemed obsessed with the topic.

McMahon's coffin shop was located along an alley just off Niagara Street and at present consisted of a good-sized workshop, a shed to one side, and a tiny yard that presently contained two wheelbarrows and a lot of snow.

Inside, it smelled of wood shavings and linseed oil. The front of the workshop was filled with coffins and they were—

Things of beauty, really.

Arrayed along one wall, they ranged from simple pine to a beauty, front and center, made from what looked like walnut. All finished with exquisite care, and highly polished.

It mattered to Liam McMahon, how the dead went to their final rest. Surely the proposed investor would see that without Ben's help.

But yes, Liam deserved a chance to show off his products to best advantage. To build a business that would benefit the city. In Ben's opinion, anything that furthered Buffalo was worth accomplishing.

The man himself came hurrying out accompanied by what must be his workers—a young, thin fellow wearing a flat cap, and a taller, broader fellow with an earnest expression. Liam had said he had three workers—the other must be off about other business.

An exquisite woman with golden hair and wide, somewhat vacant blue eyes held the hand of the big, broad fellow. She leaned into his shoulder as Liam introduced his workers as one Pete Hollins and the other Reynold Michaels, called Rey.

"My wife, Lily," Reynold said then with a shy grin. The woman leaned up and kissed him on the cheek.

"Good luck today, husband," she said fondly before looking at Liam. "Good luck, Mr. McMahon."

It was her voice that gave her away, though it was very nearly faultless. A bit too perfect perhaps, and just slightly lacking in inflection. She was a hybrid automaton. And how might a rough worker such as Michaels end up with a beautiful, hybrid wife?

Liam, making nothing of it, said merely, "Good day to ye, Lily, darlin'." And moved on to introduce his two automatons, which Ben found oddly touching.

McMahon's coffin shop, so it seemed, was more than it appeared.

"This is a thing of beauty." Ben ran his hand along the central casket. "Honestly, I don't think you need me. Your work will speak for itself."

"Still and all, I'm glad to have you here." Liam launched into some background information, how the shop had originally belonged to a man called Franz Hengerer, a German immigrant. When Franz retired, Liam, who had been his assistant, bought him out.

"The shop next door's available, if I want to expand. But like I told you, 'twill take money up front.

"And if I'm to do funerals, I'll need a proper carriage and horse." Liam laid a hand on Reynold's shoulder. "Rey and his barrow won't do any more. I'd like one o' those new, shiny steam horses, so I would, to take the dead over to Forest Lawn. But Jaysus, they're dear."

Ben nodded. He was used to gathering facts and making reports to Mitch Carter, concise and sometimes persuasive. That's what he'd do now.

But Bruce Buchanan arrived like a whirlwind, a ball of energy rolling into the shop and affecting everything in his path. Ben understood at once why McMahon felt overwhelmed by the fellow. Not that Buchanan seemed a particularly hard man, just bluff of manner and keen of eye. His gaze moved everywhere. Over the shop and its contents, over the men who worked there.

His hearty attitude, so Ben suspected, covered a shrewd discernment. He shook Ben's hand so vigorously his teeth rattled, and inspected him as closely as the premises.

"I've heard of these new funeral parlors in Europe," he said. "There are none so far in Canada—that's where I'm from. It's an interesting idea."

"You can see the quality of the product McMahon's produces," Ben told him, stroking the glorious walnut casket again. "None finer in all the city."

"Oh, no question. But pricey, eh? Mr. McMahon"— Bruce fixed Liam with a bright blue stare—"you and your workers are craftsmen. If you expand, who will be able to afford your services?"

For an instant, Liam looked taken aback. Then his Irish tongue loosened. "Well, sir, I figure we'd have different levels see, according to what folks could afford. This here's our top model, but we sell pine caskets too, still well-finished, of course. I'd never ask a customer to lay their beloved dead in an inferior casket.

"Our man here, Rey, already goes to collect the dead if they've no one to do for them, and I've been known to contribute a coffin for the destitute."

"Very admirable," Buchanan concurred.

"And I thought, why not offer similar services to those who could pay?"

Ben smiled to himself. He didn't think that once launched Liam truly needed him. The big Irishman's enthusiasm alone should carry him through.

"Well," Buchanan said, "this may only be my adopted city, but I do like investing in small businesses. I'm backing the Buffalo's Best Beer team in the upcoming hockey tournament. And I'm eager to back a growing enterprise like this one."

Liam beamed at Ben over Buchanan's head.

"Mr. Ambrose," Buchanan asked, "do you like hockey?"

"It's an exciting sport, certainly," Ben said diplomatically. "And I absolutely do like Buffalo's Best Beer."

"Who doesn't?" Bruce demanded, and they all laughed. "All right, Mr. McMahon, you have my interest. Why not tell me what you have planned for your expansion?"

Chapter Nine

The dog fussed and whined all night. Maj didn't know if that was just because he wasn't used to being shut inside or if his scruffy little body hurt. But he paced and refused for some time to settle. When he did finally drop off on the blanket Maj had provided for him on the floor, he cried and barked in his sleep.

The other residents of the Haven didn't appreciate it. First, Maj's immediate neighbors pounded on the walls. Next a group of three irate women came to Maj's door.

"Keep that mutt quiet, can't you?"

"I think he's having bad dreams." Maj added, hoping for a little sympathy, "Poor thing."

No pity was forthcoming. "You'll have to shut him up," said Mary, a fierce woman of advanced years, "or I'll speak to Mrs. Gideon about it."

I have to get my own lodgings, Maj thought as she turned back to her bed. It was not necessary for her to stay here now that Topaz was paying her a decent wage.

Besides, her room here was needed for someone less fortunate. She didn't think Topaz would ever ask her to leave, but if Maj vacated, it would mean another girl could come off the street.

The thing was, she wasn't good at saving money and didn't have much put aside. Rent was expensive, and since they'd started getting paid, automatons took up many of the available rentals.

Last summer when the plague had stalked the city, Mayor Piffin had shut everything down. City residents were ordered to stay in their homes. Only, Maj hadn't had a home back then, having parted ways with those who'd raised her some time previous. She'd been living on the streets hand to mouth—or rather, other people's pockets to mouth.

She'd met Topaz when she'd very unwisely tried to nick her purse. Topaz had caught her, turned and looked at her with those strange, amber-colored eyes of hers. Maj didn't know what Topaz had seen, but she'd been much more merciful than Maj expected.

Maj had started staying here at the Haven then. When the other girls questioned it, Topaz shrugged and said, "She's trying to get off the streets like the rest of you, just for a different reason."

Now, though, the terrible plague doctors who'd roamed the city had been caught, and the city freed from their grip. Maj had seen one of them once, and had cowered behind a row of garbage cans while it stalked by. Just thinking about it made her shiver. She walked over to the dog and picked him up in her arms.

"Little fellow," she addressed him as severely as she could manage, which wasn't very severely at all, "you have to be quiet. If Topaz hears of this, she'll never let you stay. It will be straight down to Jamie Kilter's for you."

The dog snuggled close. Maj sat on the bed, up against the pillow and settled him in her lap.

She wasn't good at saving her wages, no. She was good at spending them. On clothing, usually bright in color, that caught her eye. On baubles like the one she now wore around her neck. On dye for her hair.

It occurred to her that if she had rooms of her own she might be able to keep the pup, as Lolly called him. But she'd have to make more money than she did now.

Could she earn extra by helping—consulting with, as she supposed Topaz would call it—this Benjamin Ambrose?

Her nose wrinkled involuntarily. She didn't like the idea. And she didn't like the way he made her feel, or the sensations he raked up inside.

Dangerous.

She'd always known on some level that tapping into the energy streams she sensed running beneath the city could be risky. Especially now that the city was—well—ailing.

Potentially connecting with Benjamin Ambrose felt the same way.

She would take the pup down to Jamie Kilter in the morning. See if he had an opening, and what was what.

Till then she just had to keep the scrap of an animal quiet.

****

She went out early as she did every morning to get the newspaper for Topaz, and took the dog with her. By the time she got back to the Haven, Topaz had already arrived and her husband Romney Gideon with her.

Seeing Mr. Gideon always made Maj feel like she'd been punched in the chest. He didn't often accompany Topaz to the Haven, maybe because he caused such a stir among the girls. But he was here today.

A handsome man, and no mistake. He stood only an inch or two above Topaz's robust height and had fair hair, blue eyes, and a wealth of quiet charm.

He smiled at Maj when she came in with the newspaper—and the pup. "Who's this, then?"

"Umm, Pup."

"Another stray, eh?" Romney asked, with an amused glance at his wife.

"It won't be staying." Topaz glared. "Not if the complaints I've heard about all the noise last night continue." She glared harder. "And that better not be a name—Pup."

"I have to call him something," Maj huffed. "I'll take him down to Jamie Kilter's today, if you give me leave."

"Granted."

Romney took the paper from Maj's hand and unfolded it. "There you have it. Look at the headline."

Maj would rather not. She could read, though not well. The effort sometimes made her head hurt.

Fortunately, Romney read it out for her. "City to Prepare for Monster Blizzard."

"So I've heard. More snow? We don't need it," Topaz protested. "That's all we've had since November."

"Ah, but no, my darling wife." Romney gave her a blinding smile. "What we've had thus far was just *snow*. According to this, the weather wizards are predicting a storm of epic proportions. One of a magnitude that's seen only once or so in a hundred years."

"Oh, wonderful."

"It says people are buying quantities of coal in advance and stocking up on the essentials, like flour and butter. And beer."

"Weather's not too bad out there right now," Maj offered. "I actually saw a glint of sun through the clouds."

"Good time for you to go down to the Animal Sanctuary. And come back without that dog."

Maj fed Pup before they went, though she didn't pause to take any food for herself. Most of the sidewalks had been cleared, and yes, a watery sun shone down. All manner of traffic filled the streets, the residents no doubt taking advantage of the break in weather. Horse-drawn carts vied for space with snorting steamcabs, drays, and delivery wagons, churning the mess underfoot to mush.

Pup trembled in Maj's arms and shook still harder when they reached the shelter, where other dogs could be heard barking.

"It's all right," she whispered to him and wished she believed it. Jamie Kilter would be kind to the animal. Still—

A woman, very pretty and with a toddler at her feet and a babe in her arms, answered the peal of the bell. Jamie Kilter's wife, quite appropriately called Cat.

She gave Maj and her charge a big smile. "Another one?"

Maj struggled to return the smile. "He followed me."

"Of course. Come on in. Jamie's out back tending the crew."

By crew, Maj understood Cat meant the assorted beasts. The property had once been a small warehouse. Jamie had set up a number of kennels inside for animals that came in injured. Out back were more pens for everything from rabbits to horses. Space, though, was limited.

Cat led Maj through to the area out back where she gave a call. "Jamie?"

The yard had been cleared of snow, and all the pens,

as Maj saw at a glance, were clean. Two horses, obviously aged, were stabled on the left. A goat and a limping chicken roamed free. The dogs heralded the arrival of Maj and Pup with crazed barking, and the man tending them turned around.

He was tall and well-built, with a half-ruined face. A boiler accident when he was younger, so Maj had heard, had rendered the skin on one side red and molten-looking. Truly frightful to see.

A girl had to be prepared for the sight of Jamie Kilter.

Yet he had the most wonderful eyes, clear and blue, and they held a wealth of compassion when they focused not on Maj but on the dog in her arms.

"Another one?" he echoed his wife, who with the children had ducked back inside.

"I'm afraid so. He was trying to make his way through snow higher than his head."

"Poor mite." Jamie came over and patted the dog, still in Maj's arms. "Just one eye?" Close up, Jamie's scars were even more horrific. "It's been a terrible winter for animals in the city. Just awful. Any number of working horses have slipped and gone down. And the strays—well, with all the snow cover they can't scavenge very well, can they?"

"I suppose not. This one looked skin-and-bones when I gave him a bath. He's all fur."

Jamie's bright eyes met hers in an assessing look. It measured her emotions only. She doubted he ever really saw any woman besides his wife.

"I don't suppose you can keep him? We're pretty full up, and I'd hate to billet him out here with the big dogs."

"You think they'd pick on him?"

"I wouldn't let that happen, but it's cold for a little guy without any meat on his bones."

Maj made a face. "My employer won't let me keep him. He makes noise crying and barking at night."

"Ah. Well in that case I suppose we can squeeze him in. I'm trying to expand, but the landlord on the other side of us isn't interested in having his property occupied by dirty critters, as he calls them. I'll keep pushing."

"You're a good man, James Kilter."

"It's not for me, is it? For the animals. They have nowhere else to turn and nobody to speak for them."

"How do you think this little fellow lost his eye?"

"I hate to think." Jamie reached out and very gently parted the fluffy fur over Pup's missing eye, where the empty socket had shrunken to a seam. "Could be any number of ways. Might have injured himself, or been injured."

Maj shuddered. She tried to hand Pup over to Jamie. As much as any canine could, he clung to her, wrapping his front legs around her arm and digging in his claws. Once he was in Jamie's arms he yelped and cried.

"There now," Jamie soothed, and shot Maj another assessing glance. "Seems like he's got attached to you. You sure you want to part with him?"

Maj's gaze met Pup's single, large, imploring eye. An exchange took place.

"No. Say, could you just hold him for me temporarily? Until I can make other arrangements?"

Jamie grinned. It made him look younger. "Sure can."

Maj dug in her pocket and produced a few coins. "Here. For his keep. I'll be back for him."

"I hope so. Wouldn't want his little heart to break."

Maj tried to convey reassurance to Pup. "I'll be back. You be good now."

Pup yelped and subsided. He looked miserable.

I'll have to do whatever I can to provide for him, Maj thought as she walked home, her arms feeling dreadfully empty. Even if that did, indeed, mean taking on Benjamin Ambrose.

Chapter Ten

Ben's feet felt like blocks of ice by the time he got home that evening. In addition to his stint with Liam at the coffin shop, he'd accomplished no fewer than three tours of orphanages, taking advantage of the break in the weather. He had two more scheduled for tomorrow morning. A place called Lost Waifs and the Morgan Home for Children.

He'd tramped for miles, travel by foot still being easier than anything else and, well, less complicated than trying to ride a conveyance. His specs had iced up and his boots had failed to keep out the wet. He couldn't wait to get them off.

Winston, as always, waited for him, a familiar face, so to speak, that somewhat lifted Ben's spirits. As much as he could, Winston appeared worried.

"How are you, Master Benjamin? Have you recovered from your recent incident?"

Ben didn't suppose he had. Oh, on the surface his energies had returned, and he seemed to have overcome the longing for Clara McMahon. But deep down, he still felt like he wanted something. He just did not know what.

"Benjamin? Is that you?" Mother called from the kitchen. "I'm making the tea."

Tea would be good, the hotter the better. A drink would prove still more beneficial. Ben entered the parlor and crossed to the sideboard where he poured himself a stiff whiskey before sitting down and shucking his boots.

His socks were wet. He should go upstairs and get a dry pair. He didn't know if he had the strength.

"Winston, will you please go up and get me a pair of socks?"

"Certainly, Master Benjamin."

He heard the automaton bump his way up the stairs right before someone pealed the bell. He swore to himself and padded out, supposing the mechanical maid, Dora, must be busy helping Mother in the kitchen.

Maybe it was McMahon come to thank him for his services earlier, or to tell him the outcome of Bruce Buchanan's visit. He hauled open the door.

Not McMahon. Instead, the dying light—for it got dark early at this time of year—revealed the small figure of a woman standing on the doorstep. Magenta Rask.

Oh, hell. What is she doing here?

She jerked her head up when the door flew open. The movement failed to make her look any more imposing, since her head came only to his chin.

Not knowing what else to say, he croaked out, "Yes?"

"Mr. Ambrose? You remember me? Magenta Rask from Mrs. Gideon's Haven for Disadvantaged Women, yesterday."

How could he possibly forget her? Given that hair, the—well, he guessed he'd call it flamboyant—clothing, and the way she made him feel.

He stopped right there because he couldn't define how she made him feel. Uneasy, perhaps. Terribly on edge. Overly aware.

"Of course, Miss Rask. Come in."

"Cold out, ain't it?" she demanded as she entered, her boot heels clattering on the parquet floor of the narrow entry. She seemed as uncomfortable as he felt.

Politely, he agreed, "The weather has been vile. And I hear there's a major blizzard predicted."

"Yes, I heard that too. It was in the paper this morning."

"You don't say?" He barely knew what words he uttered. Magenta Rask was standing in his foyer. He didn't quite know what to do with her, so he gave a slight bow.

"Miss Rask, how can I help you?"

Her dark eyes engaged his. He still found that deep gaze to be unsettling, even—well, spooky. And her face—he'd never seen one like it, an odd mixture of the exotic and the elfin.

"I was hoping I could help you. What Mrs. Gideon, Topaz, talked about. I thought we might come to an agreement on payment and set up some—er—sessions."

"Benjamin? Who is it?" Mother's voice came from the kitchen. Her footsteps swiftly followed. She appeared from the back of the house, stopping in dismay when her gaze found Magenta Rask.

On the whole, Benjamin's mother possessed considerable composure. Usually the only thing that discomfited her was one of Benjamin's episodes. Now, however, her mouth fell open.

"Mother, this is Magenta Rask. Miss Rask, my mother, Beatrice Ambrose."

Mother continued to stare and said nothing.

"Good evening," Magenta told her.

"I…um…good evening."

Ben narrowed his gaze and surveyed Magenta again,

wondering just what it was about her that caused such a stricken look to enter his mother's eyes. The tall boots, perhaps, which nevertheless failed to add much to Miss Rask's diminutive height. The hair which seemed to glow an unnatural purple-red beneath the overhead lights, contrasting rather horribly with the rust-colored hat perched upon it.

Her coat matched the hat—sort of. The sleeves were rust-colored, embroidered in purple, and the tails flared out, a patchwork of different colors and textures. Like something from a circus.

"Mother, Miss Rask and I have some business— er—private matters to discuss. If you'd excuse us."

Mother goggled. "Of course."

"If you will kindly ask Winston to bring in the tea." Ben turned to Magenta. "Please, Miss Rask, come into the parlor."

She preceded him in, swiveling her head to look around as she did. "This is a nice house."

"Thank you. It was built back in 1812 after most of the city burned down."

"Sturdy and elegant." She spun to face him. "It feels—comforting."

"Ah." She must be able to sense that. And it was her ability to sense things that concerned him, right? Her capacity to help him. To find out what was amiss inside him, and maybe even what kept causing him to...die.

"Please have a seat."

She perched on the edge of a chair, but her gaze still roamed the room, measuring and evaluating. He sat on the sofa opposite her and caught her stealing a glance at his feet.

"My shoes were wet when I came in. Please forgive

me."

"It's all right. If we wind up undertaking what Topaz—Mrs. Gideon—suggested, well, there'll be a lot more between us than bare feet."

Ben cleared his throat. "I was under the impression I would contact you if I decided to go forward with the association."

"Yeah, that was the deal. But things have changed a little. So since you left your address with her and I happened to puzzle it out—"

Puzzle it out? Oh, she must not be able to read very well. Curious.

"What has changed?" he asked, but she couldn't answer because Dora came rolling in then with the tea tray, closely followed by Winston, who had a pair of Ben's socks dangling from his hand.

Could this get any more embarrassing?

Ben jerked his head at Winston. "Later." And to Dora, "Just set that down, please, and leave us."

"Do you not want me to pour the tea?" Dora seemed baffled.

"I'll do it, thanks."

"I can pour." Magenta edged forward and applied herself to the tray, which Dora had set on a low table between them. "I like playing grand lady." She poured with a flourish and eyed the assortment of biscuits on the tray. "Eee, don't they look good?"

"Please help yourself."

She did, taking one of each variety and sipping from her cup. "Oh, that is good on a cold night." Her eyes came up to meet Ben's once more, and he felt—well, that was a kind of thrill, wasn't it? Unlike anything he'd ever experienced.

"You don't mind me calling round, Mr. Ambrose?"

"I don't, and I suppose you should call me Benjamin, if we're going to work together. Are we going to work together?"

"Yes. Oh, yes." She smiled at him and it changed everything, changed her from a slightly foreign-looking stranger to one warm and utterly engaging. That smile unleashed her piquancy in full force.

"Benjamin, I intend to save you from your habit of dying."

Chapter Eleven

The Lost Waifs Home for Children appeared to be one of the smaller orphanages in the city. Ben stood at the gate with his back to Breckenridge Street and eyed it carefully, part of his assigned inspection.

There were certain things Mr. Carter wanted to know about a prospective project. In what condition was the building? How many children were in residence? Were they well cared for?

After this inspection, Ben would have to write up a report, over which Mr. Carter would pour very laboriously. So he had a checklist in his mind.

In this case the building, a large foursquare house with three stories and a cellar, could use painting, certainly nothing that could be accomplished at this time of year. The walkway and narrow drive had been carefully shoveled. The windows looked clean.

He drew a breath and squared his shoulders. The interiors of such places were often chaotic, with troubling sights and smells.

Mr. Carter poured an enormous amount of money into these improvements. Good thing he had deep pockets.

By the time Ben reached the front door of the orphanage, it opened. A small, redheaded woman in a white bib apron stood there.

"Are you Mr. Carter's inspector?" she asked with a

rich Irish brogue.

"I am." He gave her a bow. "Benjamin Ambrose."

"Daisy, let the man in."

The woman behind the girl looked neat as a pin, starched and buttoned down in a gray suit, wearing a composed expression. She extended a hand to Ben. "Mrs. Marner. I am manageress here."

"Benjamin Ambrose."

Beyond the woman, what looked like the entire staff of the place, including a line of aging steam units, stood as if waiting to greet the king or some such. In addition to the automatons and the girl who had answered the door, there was another girl with a withered arm, and a tall, dark-haired fellow. Something about the way they stood together declared they might be—well, *together*.

Mrs. Marner swiftly introduced them, going down the line. "Daisy Kilkarney, steamies Hank, Tom, Molly, Becky, Trina, and Nellie. And this is our caretaker, Kasper Czak and his wife, Tori."

Czak gave Ben a steady handshake.

"I can show you the highlights, Mr. Ambrose, and then Kasper can show you the details of the building, if you like."

"That would be grand."

A small operation and no mistake, as Ben ascertained when Mrs. Marner gave him the tour, talking all the while. Only twenty-three children in residence, and as Mrs. Marner told him proudly, each received three meals a day. They'd lost several residents to the plague last year and just acquired one more. The ground floor of the house consisted of kitchen, laundry, Mrs. Marner's office and residence, a dining room, and what they were calling a training room—formerly the parlor.

"We've recently started giving the older children—and the younger, if they are interested—training in sewing, cooking, and light repairs. It came about, actually, when we were locked down during the plague and trying to keep everyone occupied. Our staff provides the instruction, and Mr. Czak's maintenance class is very popular."

"Impressive," Ben told her, "especially for so small an operation."

She flushed. "We do not discriminate, Mr. Ambrose, between the boys and the girls. If some of the boys wish to sew, well there may be a time in the future when they are pressed to mend their own clothing. The same, if a girl wishes to pick up a hammer."

"Very advanced, Mrs. Marner."

"That's not to say we don't need help. We do, quite desperately. Lost Waifs is privately owned by a woman called Miss Radmacher. She expends the bare minimum on us. I hope that won't affect Mr. Carter's decision."

"Don't worry, Mrs. Marner. Many of the smaller orphanages we take on are privately owned. Mr. Carter often buys them outright. May I see the children?"

The second floor held three dormitories, one for boys, one for girls, and one for infants. All the children Ben saw when he peeked into the various rooms looked clean and well-cared for, enjoying some free time during his visit. The third floor held former servants' quarters that the staff had used during lockdown.

That part of the tour being completed, and with anxiety in her eyes, Mrs. Marner handed Ben off to Kasper Czak saying, "I hope, Mr. Ambrose, you find us suitable and Mr. Carter's decision will not be long in coming."

"I will make my report to him later today. Mr. Carter usually does not take too long. But it is his decision, you understand. I merely provide the facts."

She nodded, but he saw the desperation in her eyes. Last year's sickness and the accompanying lockdown had been hard on everyone. Places like this, which had barely been hanging on, were driven to the very edge.

Kasper Czak took polite charge of him and showed him the utility side of the Home—the cellar, the laundry area, the yard. Czak had a heavy accent Ben couldn't quite place, and Ben could tell Lost Waifs mattered to him. This wasn't just a job for the young man.

"I try to keep up," he confided, as they clattered down the stairs to the cellar, "but it is not easy. I sometimes think everything is on the verge of breaking. Like this steamplant."

He indicated a hulking steam boiler which lurked in the gloomy cellar amid a wealth of rust. "This powers everything, and if it goes, we cannot afford to fix it. I do not know what we would do.

"The same with the roof. With all the snow and ice up there and the guttering frozen solid, it has started backing up and leaking in. I have patched it already three times."

Ben looked at Czak with new respect. "You never went up there in this weather?"

Czak shrugged modestly. "I had to. Water was coming in. Let me show you."

They clattered all the way up to the attic where Czak pointed out water stains in some of the tiny rooms. Peering out one of the narrow windows and measuring the distance to the ground, Ben shuddered inwardly.

"Lucky you didn't slide and fall off. You are a brave

man, Mr. Czak."

"Or crazy." Kasper Czak gave a radiant smile. "That is what my wife says. I tell her, I cannot slip off." He concluded simply, "She needs me too much."

Czak watched Ben make notes before he sobered and said, "Do you think we will get the help we need? Mr. Ambrose, we are just trying to make things better for the children, and for the city."

It seemed there were a lot of people attempting to do just that. Yet the divisions, mainly between the automatons and the humans, remained.

Or perhaps that should be between those residents who supported the automatons attaining an equal footing and those who still wanted them gone.

"Was the plague bad here?" he asked Czak sympathetically.

The man nodded. "I do not know if you heard, but we who work here at Lost Waifs had a part in uncovering and exposing those who created the sickness. The same men who blamed it on the hybrid automatons." He frowned. "I love this city. I only wish it could heal."

****

Ben thought about that, about healing, after he left Lost Waifs. Was it possible for the inhabitants of Buffalo, so widely divided, to ever come together? Taken a step farther, would he ever overcome whatever ailed him, even with the help of Magenta Rask?

Magenta. All morning long he'd been unable to dismiss her from his mind. He'd lived all his twenty-five years with the possibility of dying at any time, without warning. What made him think that such a creature as she could change that?

He needed to—somehow—put her out of his mind.

He would write up his notes and recommend to Mr. Carter that he undertake the renovation of Lost Waifs. Yes, there was a lot there needing done, and it would cost a bundle.

Mitch Carter possessed a bundle, but he was shrewd about spending it. Ben would have to make his report…well, persuasive. Because he felt Lost Waifs and the people there deserved it. Not a decision he'd made clinically or even logically but by pure instinct.

The weather had cleared somewhat, though the wind remained cold, driving gray clouds overhead. As Ben paused on the corner and looked back down Breckenridge toward the river, a shaft of sunlight broke through and illuminated the air in a ladder of gold.

Whatever else happened, the world was beautiful and he certainly didn't want to leave it yet. He wanted to accomplish something, to help folks like those he'd just met. He wanted to spend time—perhaps a lot of it—with Magenta Rask.

And just like that, there she was again in his mind. He could push her out for a few moments, not for long.

Benjamin, I intend to save you from your habit of dying.

Could she? He shivered because looking ahead for an outcome to that question equated gazing into a black unknown. But he would see her tonight at a place called the Rabid Rabbit on West Tupper Street. No doubt he would find out then.

He could hardly wait.

Chapter Twelve

Perhaps it had been a bad idea—it had been Maj's suggestion after all—to meet Benjamin Ambrose here tonight. The tavern was one of Maj's haunts, had been even back when she'd survived by thievery. She felt comfortable here, and she didn't feel entirely comfortable with Benjamin.

Yet.

Whether or not she would come to feel comfortable with him remained to be seen. There was—well, something there. She couldn't yet say what.

But the Rabid Rabbit seemed curiously lively for a week night. She'd hoped they'd be able to grab a table at the back where they could, in essence, be alone and might talk privately.

She certainly couldn't take him back to the Haven. And trying to talk at his house—well, it felt so restrictive there. As if his mother might be stretching her ears to listen.

She needed to see him on level ground, though she had to admit the Rabid Rabbit might not be that.

Even though it was early in the evening, a group of what looked like laborers were already drunk, crowding the bar and singing. A little knot of toughs occupied the opposite corner and there were at least three working girls present. In the center of the floor, another group kept toasting each other, making a lot of racket about it.

Yeah, maybe she should have arranged to meet Benjamin somewhere else.

Upon that thought she saw him come in and stand for a moment as if seeking to orient himself, blinking through his wire-rimmed spectacles. He made a striking figure, if such a quiet man could be called striking. Maybe because he looked so out of place. He wore a good coat and a hat on his brown hair and he sort of oozed silent class. Might be the only person here tonight who did.

Maj got to her feet from the tiny table she'd managed to grab in a shadowy nook, and waved her hands at him. One of the disadvantages of being short was people often skipped over her.

Which of course was a good thing when engaged in thieving.

"Benjamin!"

He shouldn't have been able to hear her over the racket, yet he did. He grimaced slightly when his gaze connected with hers and fought his way across the room.

Maj watched him, wondering at what she felt inside. She barely knew this man. Except in a curious way it felt as if she did. He couldn't be more different from her, except that he wasn't.

He neared the table, and to her own surprise she reached out and clasped his hand. "Sorry to bring you here. It's probably not your kind of place."

He cast another look around the room while he removed his hat and set it on the table. "Is it yours?"

"Used to be."

He'd let go of her hand very promptly. She wondered how she felt about her grabbing hold of him like that. He sat down opposite her and eyed her drink.

"You want something to drink, Benjamin? I'll go to the bar."

He made a visible effort to relax. "Sure. What are you having?"

"A Bee Buzzler. Specialty of the house. Three kinds of whiskey. Gets you buzzed fast. I can recommend the ale here."

"Ale will be good."

She rose and wove her way to the bar, glancing back only once to see that he watched her, which gave her a little jolt of—well, satisfaction, maybe.

"It's not usually this busy in here," she said when she put the foaming mug in front of him. "Must have something to do with that hockey tournament that's coming up. A lot of people in town."

He nodded, still watching her carefully. As she'd observed previously, he wasn't what she'd call handsome. But he was nice looking. And oh, those eyes—chocolate brown and full of things she wanted to know.

She fought the desire to reach across the table and touch him again. What was the matter with her?

"Why don't you tell me," she suggested, "about this habit you have of dying? When did it start?"

He glanced around the room again.

"Don't worry, nobody will hear. It's too noisy."

"I was four the first time. It started as a tingling in my toes that spread and turned to numbness. I can still remember sitting there with my toys, feeling it happen. I tried to run and find my mother, but I didn't make it. When the—the numbness reached my chest...my heart, I guess...I died."

Goodness, just a child. She tried to recall herself at

four and failed. Cold and hungry, no doubt.

"Is it the same every time? The tingling and the numbness?"

He nodded.

"How many times have you—"

"I've lost count. Thirteen?"

An unfortunate number.

"Fourteen, fifteen. I don't know for sure. The cause is not physical. I've seen more doctors than you could shake a stick at. From way back I've been examined most thoroughly. Healthy as a horse."

"Yes. Right." It was spiritual. Maj could feel that the same way she felt the energy of the city flowing beneath her feet, waxing and waning.

"How do you get brought back?"

His eyes met hers. "Somebody intervenes. A doctor or an ambulance driver, or—well, I can't really say. If it happened when I was alone, I'm not sure I would come back."

Frightening. And a very disquieting way to live.

"Miss Rask, I don't share this with anyone lest they should think me—well, strange. Or mad. If we work together, you'll have to keep it quiet."

If. "We're going to work together. And I told you to call me Magenta. Or Maj. How do you feel when you come out of one of these episodes?"

"Awful." One side of his mouth quirked up. "Like I've been dead."

"Yes, well, we'll have to get to the bottom of it. But we'll need a place to meet. A—a private place where no one can interrupt us. I'm thinking of moving out from the Haven, but I'll need to pay the rent up front, you see? If I had a place, we could meet there." And she could go get Pup from Jamie Kilter's.

Behind the wire-rimmed spectacles, Benjamin Ambrose's steady gaze rested on her. He appeared calm, but she could sense so much going on beneath the surface. A veritable storm of emotions.

"Let me ask you this, Maj. Do you have a genuine desire to help me, or do you just wish to earn some money?"

Both. She said it aloud. "Both." She gave in to the impulse and clasped his hands. Her fingers tingled where they touched his, and inside she felt—

Ah, there were no words for it. *Thrilled* came close. Or maybe *overmastered.*

What would happen if she kissed him? It would be like dipping her lips into molten fire.

Again, he pulled his hands from hers. If he sensed what she did, it seemed he did not welcome it. Perhaps he didn't get touched often. Or maybe she, with her puce-colored hair and outlandish clothing, merely repelled him.

He reached into the pocket inside his coat. "I brought some money in case we came to an agreement. Mother and I don't have much, but there is a fund for my—er—emergencies, set up by my father long ago." He paused with his hand in the air. "Do you think you can help me?"

"Yes."

"You're not just saying that to—to earn a fee?"

"I'm not just saying that." Maybe she had been unsure at the start. But not now that she'd been in his company. Had touched him…

She leaned closer. "I can sense things, you see. What's inside people. Animals. The city itself. I can feel whether things are right inside them."

"Can you sense what's inside me?"

She placed the flat of her hand against his chest. This time he tolerated her touch, and she closed her eyes, shutting out the racket around them and all the other distractions bombarding her.

She could feel him. Like a river of energy. Deep and dark, marked with bright sparks of light in a chain. There were breaks in that chain of light, forces working to disrupt it. He needed—

He needed her.

She gasped and her eyes flew open. How could she tell him such a thing? This rather staid and steady man.

With a propensity to die.

Panic fluttered in her gut. She could not tell him that. Neither could she let him walk away from her.

"I can help you, Benjamin Ambrose."

For an instant the golden light that was within him flickered in his eyes. "How?"

"I can't explain that here."

An argument had broken out across the room, men shouting at each other. About who should pay for the drinks, probably. Or which hockey team they were backing. Or whether automatons were good or evil. Could be any damn thing.

She stared into his eyes. "You'll just have to trust me." An absurd statement. For most her life, she'd been utterly untrustworthy.

His hands came up and clutched her hand, still planted against his chest. She expected him to pluck it off. Instead he pressed it closer. His heartbeat came through his clothing and into her flesh right along with all that streaming energy.

"I can feel you," she whispered.

"I can feel you too."

A blast from a steam cannon erupted in the room. At first Maj thought it was part of what she was getting from Benjamin. Then a second blast scorched the opposite wall. It was coming from the door.

A couple had entered the tavern, and even among the uproar that filled the place they commanded attention. The man because he was over six feet of strapping, handsome, er, policeman. He wore the uniform but with the bright brass buttons of his coat undone and his braces showing.

The woman—Maj blinked. Tall with a wealth of rich chestnut hair that flowed over her shoulders, she wore a costume even more outlandish than Maj's own, a fringed jacket and a skirt short enough to show off her high, tooled-leather boots. It was she who brandished the sidearm, a small, neat steam cannon that made Maj long for one of her own.

Even as Maj—along with everybody else there— stared, she raised it high and sang out, "Everybody settle down! There'll be no blood shed here tonight, though a few of you might get singed. Arthur, clear the way."

An aged and quite large steam unit rumbled past her and her partner, toward the bar. Clearly rebuilt at some point in his existence and rather crudely made, he had been polished to a high gleam with, of all things, a coat of arms painted on his chest just above the hopper.

The armed woman followed him, trailed by the copper. Maj usually kept her distance from policemen, but she'd seen this big hunk of an Irishman before, and she followed him with her eyes. "What are they doing here?"

"That's Brendan Fagan," Benjamin supplied. "Captain in the Buffalo Police Force."

"I know."

"I've met him while out on orphanage business. And she must be his lady. She's the daughter of Dr. Candace Landry. You've heard of her?"

Ah yes, the name was familiar. "Was she that woman who created all the hybrid mechanical prostitutes?" They'd been meant to spare the kind of women Topaz helped get off the streets. But it turned out the hybrids, being highly specialized, adaptable mechanicals, had minded being sold, just like the women.

"She works with automatons now," Benjamin said. "Like the one she's with. That's not going to go over well in here."

"No. This is a haven for steam-haters, it is. There's bound to be a riot in about three minutes. Time enough for us to get out. Drink your ale."

Somewhat to her surprise, he chugged it down. She tossed back the last of her Bee Buzzler too.

"Come on."

"Wait." He shoved the bundle of money, which he'd placed on the table, into her hand. "So you can rent a place we can meet. We're agreed?"

She tucked the money safe inside her jacket, wove her fingers through his, and hauled him away from the table, even as chaos broke out behind them. "Oh yes, we are." Good and agreed.

Chapter Thirteen

Outside the Rabid Rabbit, Ben paused and drew a breath. Raucous sound spewed from the place, so loud he could almost see it like a glare of light. Something bad was going to happen. Maybe that woman—Brendan Fagan's lady—and the off-duty police captain himself could corral it.

Ben never set foot in such places and only rarely consumed a pint of ale. Some sort of madness had seized him. But no—that was just Magenta's hand, the fingers woven through his as if she would never let go.

She was so small and so—so *vibrant* he supposed was the word. So disconcerting in the way he could *feel* her presence. She tugged at his hand, urging him off away from the tavern. They stepped into a cold fierce enough to sting.

People still made their way into the Rabid Rabbit. No one else had come out. Peering back, Ben asked, "Do you think she'll burn the place down?"

"Maybe. At least that'll create some warmth. Come on."

Magenta pulled him into the shadows, stopped, and faced him. She peered up and up into his face as if examining it.

"You have foam on your lips. From the ale."

"Do I?"

Before he could say anything more, she rose onto

her tiptoes and kissed him. Her lips felt soft and warm in the stinging cold, and her tongue—

Her tongue came out and collected the foam from his lips.

For an instant, shock incapacitated him. The heat of her kiss melted the shock and he sort of flowed into her, closed his arms around her and lifted her up so she didn't have to strain. She tasted like three kinds of whiskey and pure woman.

His world came right. For the first time in his entire life, it did. This—*this* was more than a physical connection, though it encompassed the physical. More than sensation. It reached deep into him, and deeper still.

The kiss went on and on. Ben forgot to breathe and then forgot what it meant to breathe. Maybe he died and came back yet again.

The tingling had similar properties. But the heat made a shield against the chill. He could feel Maj, everything inside her. He could feel it coming into line with him.

At last she drew her lips from his, gasping. Her breath, warm and sweet, gusted across his cheek. They clung to one another like two drowning souls on the same life raft.

"Umm," Ben said brilliantly, and kissed her again. She opened for him and he fell into her, barely noticing when she wound her arms around his neck and hiked herself up, wrapped her legs around his thighs.

Well, his body must have noticed, because his hands slid down unasked to boost her fanny, and he grew hard as iron.

"Take it in an alley!" Somebody roared, near at hand. Two men headed for the tavern were laughing at them. A second later, another steam cannon blast lit the interior of the Rabid Rabbit.

"We'd better get out of here, Benjamin. Benjamin—"

"Do you have that money?"

"In my vest pocket."

"Good. Then you can secure a room."

"And we can—" She nipped at his lower lip and his head spun. They would be together. They would lie together. It was inevitable.

Carefully, he set her on her feet.

"I can't procure a permanent rental right away, though, Benjamin. Perhaps we can rent a room just for tonight."

"Ah." He tingled all over but not as if he prepared to die. Maybe, this time, as if he prepared to live. "Is that really where you want it to happen, in some cheap room?" Most ladies, as he'd surmised—at least if they weren't prostitutes—required some measure of romance. Flowers. A fancy dinner or two. A proposal of marriage.

Magenta Rask said, "I don't care, so long as it happens. I know a place. Come on."

He never later knew where they went and could not have found the place again. She led and he followed. The noise fell away behind them and a few snowflakes tumbled down.

"Here."

The house was tall and narrow, not unlike his own on Virginia Street, with a sign out front that read merely, *Rooms*.

"Let's hope they have something left."

"Is this a flop house?"

"No, a rooming house. It's clean."

She tugged him up the walk through trodden snow. The bell sounded loud when she rang it.

"What you want?" The voice, through a slot, sounded unfriendly.

"A room."

"How long?"

Magenta glanced at Benjamin, a question and an assessment, before she replied. "All night."

Oh lord, sweet heaven, oh—

The door opened. A palm appeared. "Four bits."

Magenta paid from the money he'd given her.

"Up the top of the stairs on the far right. The door that's open."

Ben never saw his hostess. Magenta pulled him up the stairs by the hand, clattering. And giggling.

Inside the room, which like the house was narrow and plain, she closed the door and turned to face him.

"Take off your coat."

The room felt chilly and a measure of sanity was filtering in. Where was he? What was he about to do?

She peeled his coat off him and kissed him again. She plucked the spectacles from his face and placed them on a table, following it with still another kiss. He ceased caring where he was.

He cradled her face between his hands so he could kiss her more deeply, pushing his fingers up into the wild mass of her unruly hair.

"Your hair—"

"Ain't natural. You'll see. When I take everything off."

He nodded dumbly and stood watching—his vision just a little blurry—while she did exactly that. Her clothing appeared complicated and came off in bits. So he saw different parts of her in turn. Her legs, when the skirt and petticoat fell. Her shoulders when the jacket came off. Her breasts when the blouse and chemise she wore beneath it followed. Her nipples were dark and beautiful, and they peaked in the cool air. She was small and perfect and—

Naked, she pressed herself against him, gazed into his face with those black eyes which now held demand.

"Your turn."

His tongue seemed to be stuck to the roof of his mouth. It stayed there while he stepped away from her and shucked his shoes, his jacket, his tie, and all the other responsible trappings he should have said made him who he was.

Funny, but with all the clothing gone, he felt more *him* than he'd ever been. Once more, she pressed herself against him, skin to skin this time. "Am I too much of a wild child for you, Benjamin?"

"No. I think you're just right."

He picked her up and carried her to the bed, a pertinent part of him so hard he felt surprised he could walk.

"Well, then." She caressed his face. "Well, then, here we are."

"Yes."

"Let's see what's what."

She kissed him and reality, including the room and its contents, flew away. Sensation flooded in. He was immersed in a river with a strong current, one he could do nothing but allow to carry him. Part of the river came from Maj and part from him, and the two parts joined together into something—well, strong and magnificent.

She touched him all over with those small hands

while their mouths remained joined. Then she broke the kiss and ran her mouth everywhere. *Everywhere.* The energy sparked and danced within him and grew into an unstoppable surge. When she took him in her mouth, he couldn't help but convulse.

She slid back up his body and gazed into his eyes.

"I—" he babbled. "I—I couldn't keep from—"

"Nor I. I climaxed too, though you probably couldn't tell. See?" She captured his hand and carried it to that hottest, most private part of her, coaxed his fingers inside. Her black eyes narrowed to slits.

"Oh."

"Yes. I hope you don't think we're done."

"No." He was going to die here tonight. For good.

His hand still inside her, she guided his lips to her breast. Small and utterly perfect in shape and form, each of them would likely fit in his mouth. He set out to test the theory.

The current that flowed through him, that flowed through both of them, once more became a flood, unstoppable.

"I want you inside me. Now."

He slid in and what remained of his life shattered. He began to move with abandon, giving to her, and taking in equal measures. He didn't remember climaxing this time. He was lost in the river, the one that answered every need.

And completed him.

When he regained his sanity—who knew how much later—he was still inside her. She had her cheek pressed to his and her arms wrapped around him as if she held on for dear life.

"No. Don't move."

"Magenta. That was—"

"I don't think there are words. Never been invented for that."

Probably not.

She lifted her cheek from his. Across a distance of mere inches, he gazed into her eyes. Those black eyes no longer frightened him, now that he knew what lay behind them.

She smiled slowly, and it was the smile of an imp. "Benjamin Ambrose, you're an imposter. You look all staid and proper. Inside, you're just as wild as me."

"Quite possibly."

"Have you been keeping all that pent up inside? No wonder you keep on dying."

"You think that's the problem, do you?"

"If so"—she nipped his lip—"I've got the cure."

"I don't think this is the sort of therapy Topaz Gideon had in mind."

"It's what I've got in mind. Any objections?"

"If I objected, I truly would be mad."

"I need to find a flat or at least a set of rooms. As quick as possible. Then you, me and Pup can all be together."

"You want me to move in with you?"

"Of course I want you to move in with me."

Ben wondered what his mother would say. He found he didn't care.

"Magenta—"

"Maj. Call me Maj."

"Maj—what I felt when we were, well, joined together—what was that?"

"I'm not sure. But it was powerful, wasn't it?"

"Have you ever felt anything like that before?"

"Never with a person. A few times when I connected with the energy that lies under ground."

"The—"

"There are streams of it. Here in Buffalo, they're like the spokes of a wheel. They run beneath some of the streets. It's a very special place, this city."

"And it feels like what we just did?"

"A little bit. The closest I've ever felt to what we just did. What you and I have is better. It's—well, it's everything, isn't it?"

Everything. That was as good a term as any.

Because he had no words, he kissed her. And felt the power rise again.

When the kiss ended, she smiled. "Good thing you're strong and healthy. Like a horse."

"Oh, yes?"

"Yes. Because by the looks of things, we'll be going all night."

Chapter Fourteen

"I thought you were dead!" Ben's mother howled the words at him, in overt distress. "I thought you must be lying somewhere out in the city. In the cold. *Dead*."

Ben stood in the middle of the entry where she'd caught him when he came in this morning. The fact was, she'd fallen upon him the way a ravening wolf might fall on a carcass. He hadn't even had a chance to remove his coat.

He remembered Magenta standing in front of him only a short time ago, smoothing the lapels of this same coat while gazing up at him. The look in her eyes had been—well, quite frankly possessive.

He had the distinct impression that two separate parts of him had just crashed together. The surface part, and that beneath.

"I'm sorry, Mother. I should have thought. I should have sent word." Truth, but who could think of such a thing while Maj ran her mouth all over his body?

"Where were you?" Mother demanded. "All night. I was preparing to call the police this morning. I did speak to the neighbors."

"The neighbors?"

"Well, to Liam McMahon. He suggested you'd gone out for a drink and had a few too many." She looked shocked. "I assured him you never do that."

Oh, hell. He should have thought. Why had she

dragged McMahon into it?

Dora came rumbling out from the kitchen and stood watching the scene.

"Where were you?" Mother cried again.

"I stayed with a friend. We met up at a tavern, as chance would have it. And since it grew late, I decided not to make my way home through the cold. I apologize, Mother. I should have sent a message."

Her eyes fairly bugged out. "A friend? Which friend?"

Not wishing to lie to her, Ben didn't answer.

"Was it Matthew Dudley, from school? I thought about sending a message to him, but you haven't said you'd seen him in some time—"

"It doesn't matter who it was."

Her eyes narrowed. "I think it does."

"I believe I have a right to my privacy."

She recoiled slightly. "In ordinary circumstances I would agree. But yours are not ordinary circumstances. I feared—"

"I am here. Whole and well. Let that be an end to the discussion. I need to change and get to work."

Clearly in a huff, Mother said, "You'll have to look at Winston first."

"Winston? What's wrong with Winston?"

"I do not know. I sent him out last evening to retrace your route from Prospect Avenue here. When he came back he was—well, gone haywire."

"Haywire?"

"Not operating correctly. See for yourself. He's in the parlor."

That room felt cold when they entered, and Benjamin experienced a stab or remorse. Mother—and

Winston and Dora—must have been terribly worried at his absence, to neglect something so basic as heat.

Winston stood at the end of the sofa beside the hearth. At first Benjamin thought he was shut down, but he stirred feebly when Ben came in.

"Winston?"

"Master Benjamin, I am glad you are back. I—" The unit jerked his arms and began to babble. "Snow. Steamcab. Absence. Death. Blizzard. Manufactured in 1862. Destruction—"

"Winston?" Swiftly, Ben crossed to the unit. "What is amiss?"

Winston's painted gaze could not meet Ben's, yet seemed to yearn toward him. "I do not know. My fire is burning well. Sufficient water, sufficient coal. Misfire. Misfire."

"Oh." The unit was old, and any number of circuits could fail. He was, however, much more to Ben than a mere mechanical. "We will need to get you looked at by someone."

"A physician?"

"A mechanic." Ben did have Winston overhauled every year by a shop called Bog and Ed's Steam Units. He wondered now if there were better repair shops in the city. "I will find the best place for you and arrange for you to be seen, hopefully today. Meanwhile, you rest."

Winston jerked around to face him more fully. "You will not shut me down?"

"I will not."

"It would be most disconcerting."

"I will not shut you down. I promise. You rest quietly here today."

"You will come back for me?"

"I will."

Mother had watched this exchange from the doorway. "Benjamin, I still want to know—"

"I can't talk now. I have to change clothes and get to work."

She moved aside silently and let him pass. "You will come home later?"

"Yes, Mother, of course I will."

****

He had inspections at two orphanages scheduled for that morning. He stopped in at Prospect Avenue first and wrote up his reports for yesterday's inspections, including the one at Lost Waifs, which he slanted in their favor. He left them for Mr. Carter, who was not yet in his office.

Outside, the weather looked deceptively quiet. He wondered if the predictions of a blizzard had been over-exaggerated. In light of all that had happened, he'd lost track of exactly when that was supposed to hit.

In light of all that had happened.

The streets remained slushy and he saw two carriages and a heavily-loaded beer wagon stuck on corners. Down near the river, where his first inspection was located, there were banners for the upcoming hockey tournament, sponsored in part by Buffalo's Best Beer.

He'd likely never be able to taste ale—or beer—again without thinking of Magenta. Remembering how she'd licked the foam from his lips. Remembering all that had come after.

No matter how he tried that morning, he couldn't get her out of his head. While he should have been compiling notes on the conditions of the buildings he saw and the welfare of the children, he was focused instead on the scent of her hair and the silky softness of her skin. The taste of her, and how it felt when she ran her hands down his body. How, when he touched her, everything inside him seemed to come right.

Funny, because she was nothing like any woman he might have chosen for himself. Too outlandish. Too—too everything. And yet even with the greatest effort he couldn't drag his thoughts from her.

He got back to Mitch's office on Prospect around noon, intending to write up more reports. As soon as he came in, Mitch Carter stuck his head out of his office.

"Benjamin? You have a visitor."

"A visitor? Me? Here?"

"I'm as surprised as you are. It's—" Mitch hesitated only marginally, "a lady."

"Oh?"

"We put her in the parlor."

"Oh?" It seemed to be all Ben could say.

"Ambrose, this is a place of business, as well as my home. Not a meeting house."

"I'm sorry, Mitch. I'm sure it won't happen again."

"See that it doesn't."

His heart hammered as he entered the parlor, an exquisite room decorated in the best of taste. Because he knew already who he would see.

She stood near the tall windows looking out front. Watching for him? Maybe, but he'd come in the back. She wore green today, a flared skirt and tight-fitting jacket all covered with what must be little, imitation jewels in rainbow colors. She'd piled her wild mop of hair on top of her head. It didn't make her look any taller.

The breath gusted from him and she turned. Before

he could speak, she ran to him and grabbed hold, her hands moving from his lapels to his cheeks and sliding down his arms. Feeling, feeling him as if making sure he was there.

Once again, everything inside him snapped into place.

"Maj," he began, "you shouldn't be here."

"I know. I know, I'm sorry. I had to see you."

She kissed him and he promptly lost all his worry, his distress, and his longing. He closed his hands around her waist and drew her closer. The scent of her enfolded him.

By God. By God!

The kiss ended slowly, reluctantly, and with tenderness. He realized he was standing in his employer's parlor in the middle of the day, kissing a woman as if he could not live without her.

"How did you find me?"

"You said you work for Mitch Carter. I asked around."

"This is his home. You shouldn't—"

"I know." She repeated, "I had to see you. I just—" She gave a funny little shrug, "had to."

He nodded.

She ran her palms over him again, up his chest, around his neck, and he felt her as if he were naked once more. "I needed to make sure—" Something glinted in her black eyes. "Make sure it was all real."

"Yes. It's real."

"It is," she agreed. "Will I see you later? I have to see you later."

"Yes, but there are complications. When I didn't come home last night, my mother thought I'd died again."

"Oh. It must be, well, interesting to have a mother who keeps track of you."

"Don't most people?"

She twitched. "I don't remember mine."

"And now my steamie's broke down. He's not just a steamie, he's, well, like family."

"You should take him to Pike's. It's the best in the city. Let's meet up later. I can accompany you there, you and your steamie."

"Winston."

"Winston. That way I'm sure to see you."

"All right."

"I've spent the morning searching for a flat. I couldn't find one." She whispered, "I need to be with you again."

He thought about the impossibility of it. Mother. And Winston. Excuses and complications. He thought of Magenta naked, her breast at his lips. "Maybe."

She drew his head down so she could whisper in his ear. "I need you inside me."

Like a madman, he babbled, "Meet me at five o'clock at my house. You remember where it is?"

She nodded.

"We'll drop Winston off and then—"

He had no idea what he would tell his mother. And gazing into Magenta's dark eyes, he didn't care.

Chapter Fifteen

Magenta looked at herself in the foggy mirror of her room at the Haven and wondered about her appearance. She frequently did so, but only with a passing sort of concern. Was her clothing bright enough? Cutting-edge enough? Could her hair be a more unusual color?

Now, rather shockingly, she wondered how Benjamin Ambrose saw her. Him, so staid and reserved. And her, right there inside him.

Just like he'd got inside her.

She'd never experienced anything like it. Wholly unexpected. Unbelievable. One night and she was addicted to the man.

She tweaked at a mahogany-colored curl at her temple. He would take her as she was. Because under the surface, in the place where their living spirits ebbed and flowed, they were the same.

She'd attended a lecture once—because she did like to improve herself, having had very little formal education—where a scientist had been speaking. He'd said that all matter, the world and everything in it, was made up of pure energy. That nothing they could see or touch was real, just illusions created by that energy, vibrating very, very fast.

When she touched Benjamin Ambrose, she felt that energy as if she stuck her whole body in it.

It felt so much like what she experienced when she

connected with the energy that flowed beneath the city, it made her believe the scientist all over again.

She'd see Ben soon. At his house.

On her way out of the center, she encountered Topaz.

"Topaz, I wanted to let you know I'll be moving out just as soon as I can find a set of rooms."

Topaz's eyebrows flew up. "Should I be offended?"

"Not at all. I'm very grateful to you for having let me stay here. It's just that I've met a man and I want—need—to live with him."

Now Topaz frowned. "A man. I hope you're being sufficiently cautious and not letting your impulses run away with you."

Her impulses were, at the moment, wild horses foaming at the mouth. "It's good. I just need to find a room."

"Have you tried the automatons?"

"Eh?"

"They've been buying up a lot of property."

"I know. But don't they only rent to other automatons?"

"Sometimes, but," Topaz smiled, "they do not discriminate as much as the rest of the population. And often they charge very reasonable rent. Do you know Pat Kelly?"

"Everybody knows him. But," Maj shivered, "he's a cop."

"A member of the Irish Squad. He also heads the Automaton Liberation League. If you go there, he should be able to tell you what properties are available."

"Thank you. I'll do that. And then you'll be able to give my room here to someone else."

"So long as you keep working for me."

"Oh yes, I will. It's good work."

There were, in fact, as she thought while she made her way out to meet Benjamin, many people doing good work in the city. Topaz and this Pat Kelly, obviously, and folks like Mitch Carter who'd made quite an impression on her earlier today. And Jamie Kilter with his care for distressed animals, and the folks who tried to treat the steamies fairly. The city fair brimmed with people trying to improve it.

Then there was the darker element, the underbelly so to speak, who talked up hate, who battered steam units on dark corners, and fermented riots. It was like what flowed beneath the city itself—both thriving and sick-like. Akin to what was inside Benjamin.

And if she admitted it, herself.

She had a lot of dark inside her. She'd been part of that underbelly. Thieving, hiding, distrusting. Dwelling on her differences, which let her feel too much hate.

Now she could feel Ben and it all came right.

Seemed only fitting that he lived in the respectable part of town, just off Elmwood. It was a lovely house, as she'd observed before, even with snow heaped up all around it. It had two stone pillars out front and a stained glass light above the door.

Hoity toity.

Benjamin's mother, Mrs. Ambrose, would not be welcoming. She hadn't been, last time. And if she was angry about Maj having kept Ben away all last night— Did she know Ben had been with her?

She pealed the bell, telling herself she wasn't nervous. What was this, compared to breaking into some rich toff's house in the dead of night?

The automaton maid who'd brought the tea before answered the door. Ben was right behind her. "Maj? Come in, come in. I'm almost ready to leave."

He reached out for her hand as if he felt what she did, the sheer need to connect.

"Just let me say goodbye to Mother first."

"All right." Anything, to be with him. "Have you told her—"

"Not yet. Come in."

A steam unit stood in the parlor.

"Is this Winston?"

"Yes. He's running but appears to be misfiring somehow. Winston, this is Miss Magenta Rask. She's very important to me."

Maj flushed with pleasure. She didn't realize someone else had entered the room behind her.

"She is, is she?"

Maj spun.

Ben's mother stood stiffly, as if all up on her high horse, and full of dignity. He looked a little like her, Maj had to acknowledge. They had the same brown hair and the same air of strict-respectability. She wore a sober, dark gray dress and, just like Ben, a pair of wire spectacles.

As well as a disapproving expression.

"Mother, you remember Magenta Rask. Magenta, my mother, Mrs. Beatrice Ambrose."

"Uh—" Mrs. Ambrose choked out.

"Pleased to see you, Mrs. Ambrose."

"Benjamin." Mrs. Ambrose switched frantic eyes to Ben. "Is this the friend with whom you spent last night?"

"Yes, Mother, it is."

"Oh!"

Magenta liked that he was forthright, but his mother looked as if someone had just chucked a full piss pot at her feet.

"And I may spend tonight with her also. We'll drop Winston off at Pike's Repair Shop, and then—" He quirked a brow at Maj.

"We will spend some time together," Maj concluded.

Mrs. Ambrose appeared to be stricken silent.

"So you needn't worry," Ben added. "I shall be perfectly all right. Magenta, will you please help me roll Winston out?"

They trundled the unit between them past the silent woman, into the entry and past the other steam unit to the door. Winston was an extremely heavy unit. When they paused before taking him out, Maj realized Mrs. Ambrose had followed Ben.

"Benjamin," she spoke into her son's ear, "is this woman a prostitute?"

"No, I am not." Maj had excellent hearing. "Though I do work with a number of them. I've never sold myself and don't intend to. I used to be a thief, however, so I suppose you will consider that just as bad."

An ugly flush suffused Mrs. Ambrose's face.

For the first time, Ben's demeanor cracked. He looked mightily distressed when he said, "Mother, please try and understand. This has nothing to do with you."

"Has it not! I've looked after you all your life. And now you think you can just walk away?"

Maj raised her hand from Winston's arm. "He's grown now and don't need looking after, ma'am. If he does, well, I'm here."

They rolled Winston down the stairs between them

and along the walk, in profound silence.

It couldn't feel good, walking away from your mother that way. Maj couldn't really know since she'd never had a mother, but she could sense Ben's distress.

"He ain't going to roll easy through this snow," she said when they reached the curb. "Not all the way to Pike's."

"We need a cart or some such."

"Here. Let me."

Maj ran out into the street, where she flagged down the next conveyance that passed, a large dray pulled by two horses. The driver drew up, staring at her in astonishment, and they had a conversation.

"Can we load up my friend's automaton? We're heading that way." She pointed.

"For two bits."

Maj dug the coins from her pocket. With considerable difficulty, she and Ben tipped the heavy unit into the open back, and followed him on.

The wagon, filled with lumber and other building supplies, smelled strongly of sawdust. Maj perched beside Ben on a pile of boards.

"You all right?"

"I've never done anything like that to her before."

So she imagined.

"You've broken out, that's what you've done, Ben. You've broken out good and proper."

His gaze slid to her. "You'll look after me now, will you?"

"If you need it. Which you won't. What I was thinking was, we'll look after each other from now on."

Chapter Sixteen

Pike's Steam Repair lay down an alley on a back street off the heavy thoroughfare of Niagara Street. The carpenter's dray dropped them off on Niagara, and they had to trundle Winston the rest of the way.

Fortunately, traffic had beaten down most of the snow, and the alley had been cleared. Still, Ben and Maj were both breathless when they reached the door of the shop.

"Go ahead," Maj told Ben. "Knock."

His rap was answered by a steam unit. Aged and dented, it took in the sight of them standing with Winston between them.

"Sir? Madam? You have a unit for repair?"

"Who is it, Mordred?"

A man appeared behind the steam unit, wiping his hands on a shop rag. Of medium height, he had brown hair and keen gray eyes, and wore a long leather apron.

"You just caught me. We're getting ready to close. Who do we have here?"

"This is Winston."

"Bring him in."

The interior of the shop assaulted Ben's senses with heat, the smell of steam, and the raw tang of oil and coal smoke. Automatons and bits of automatons lay everywhere—on a large bench to the left of the door and another smaller bench on the right. Many stood posed around the perimeters of the room in various states of repair.

One of these moved when they came in, and Ben stared. He was huge, hulking and wide, with glaring red eyes.

"Uh—" he said.

"That's just Dammit, one of my assistants."

"Dammit?"

"Don't worry about it. I'm Lionel Pike. What can I do for you?"

"It's Winston. I've had him—well, just about forever, and I've done my best to keep him running. Usually I have him serviced at Bog and Ed's, but I hear you're the best in the city."

"What's happened to him?"

"He was fine when I left the house. My mother sent him out on an errand, and when I came home and he was as you see him. Barely mobile and talking gibberish. You can see he's running, but—"

"Yes." Pike peered at Winston. "Quite an old unit, but that's all right. We rather specialize in those."

"I promised I'd never shut him down."

Lionel Pike smiled for the first time. "We specialize in that too. Right, Mordred?"

The automaton who'd answered the door perked up. "I am myself most ancient. Despite that, Master Lionel does his best not to shut me down. He keeps me running at peak performance."

Feeling considerable relief, Ben nodded.

Maj's gaze moved everywhere. "This place is amazing."

"We rebuild a lot of vintage units here, the ones that might otherwise have gone to the scrap yard, and send them out to service."

Mordred put in, "It is a steamie's most fervent wish, to be of use."

Ben looked at Winston. The unit gazed back at him silently. "It's as if he's frozen. Trapped. Can you fix him?"

"Can't make any promises till I get in there, sir. Under what owner name should we tag him?"

"Oh—I'm Benjamin Ambrose." Ben belatedly stuck out his hand. "And this is Magenta Rask, my—lady."

That won another smile from Pike, and a glowing look from Maj. Pike shook his hand heartily.

"Winston will be in safe hands."

"And you won't shut him down?"

"We'll do our best not to." Pike glanced at Mordred. "The repairs may take some time. With the weather and all, we're behind."

"How long?"

"Depends on what we find. Availability of parts. How other jobs go."

Mordred said confidingly, "Master Lionel used to stay and work late every evening. All hours. But since he married, he prefers to go home."

A strange sound came from the hulking unit. It took Ben a moment to realize he was chuckling. "As do we all."

A mad place, Ben thought as he croaked out, "Well, then. I suppose I'll have to make do without him for as long as it takes." He wondered if he could. He'd never before lived without Winston.

Of course, he'd never before turned his back on Mother, either. His life changed so fast he couldn't keep up with it.

"Winston will be safe here," Mordred assured him. "And may make a few new friends."

Ben nodded and turned to Winston. "I'll be back for you no matter what. All right?"

The wind seemed to bite more sharply when they left the shop. Ben stood there in the alley for a minute trying to find his center.

Maj took his hand. "He'll be all right. It had a good feel in there, didn't it?"

Ben nodded. "Strange. But good."

"Winston's off on an adventure. So are we." She leaned up and kissed him. The confusion inside him eased and his emotions came into line. He centered, even though it might be on a new center.

"Come on. I have a list."

"Eh? A list?"

"I stopped by earlier to see Patrick Kelly, and he gave me a list of properties for rent, owned by automatons. A few of them aren't far from here. I thought you might help me choose."

"You want me to?"

"Sure. We're going to be sharing the place most of the time, aren't we?"

Ben stepped down the alley and directly into his new life.

****

He found Maj's enthusiasm irresistibly infectious. She towed him from property to property all down her list, where they viewed rooms and sets of rooms of every description.

She found something to like in each of them. The tiny ones, she dubbed cozy. The empty ones had potential and the gloomy ones just needed a bit of brightening up.

Through her eyes, Ben found he could see it all. The two of them sitting at a table that did not yet exist, sharing a pot of tea. Cozied up beside a fire. Sharing a bed.

He'd never realized how many properties were owned by automatons, many of them hybrids. Their hosts politely showed them the rears and attics of partitioned houses. None pressed them for a decision.

"You have to help me choose," Maj said at last. "They're all what I'd call reasonably priced."

"It's up to you."

"I keep thinking I'll know it when I see it."

And then she did. At the top of a very tall house on Congress Street, at the end of a staggering staircase in an attic unit, she stood and made a slow turn.

The landlord, a hybrid automaton and, Ben suspected, a member of the Irish Squad, waited at the door and watched her, even as did Ben.

She closed her eyes and put out her arms. "Ah."

Ben had never before seen anyone select a dwelling by feel. But he knew. The rooms—there was a sitting room, bedroom, and tiny kitchen, as well as a pocket-sized toilet—had ceilings that sloped with the rafters and tall, narrow windows that looked out on two sides.

Moreover, it was furnished with the bare necessities. A pair of overstuffed chairs and a table in the parlor area, a small dining table. A bed in the other room, and even a kettle on the coal stove.

Maj stopped spinning and opened her eyes. "Ben, what do you think?"

He thought the tortuous staircase made it an awfully long way to carry everything up, including loads of coal.

"Can we afford it?" he asked softly, though he figured the hybrid could hear everything.

"With what you've given me and what you and I both earn, I think so, yes."

Maj wanted the place. Ben could see that in her eyes. He could feel it inside her, like a buoyant current of rising air.

"I usually ask for a security payment," the hybrid said. "But since I like you, such a nice young couple, I'll forego that."

"Oh! That's very kind, isn't it, Ben? Shall we take it?"

What could he say? "As you like."

All enthusiasm, Maj turned to their landlord. "If I pay you for the first month's rent now, could we possibly have the place for tonight?" She glanced at Ben. "It's fiscally wise, that. It will save us the price of a room."

Ben's pulse kicked up. He too looked at the landlord.

"To be sure, miss. The place is yours from the minute you put the rent in my hand."

Maj dug the wad of money out from her bodice and counted carefully. When she handed the money to the landlord, he passed her two keys. "One is for the outside door and the other for this one."

Maj closed the door carefully when he left. She chortled as she held up the keys. "It's ours."

Yours, he wanted to say, but he knew that wouldn't be right. It was his too, if she was here. This new reality in which he moved demanded it.

He turned to the window and looked out. The house being one of the tallest on the street, he could see for blocks and blocks. Snow stretched everywhere. In the distance he could just see the gleam of the river.

He started when Maj moved into his arms. "This is what you want, isn't it? It's all right?"

"Yes. It's what I want."

She tipped her head toward the waiting bedroom. "There's a big bed in there. Want to christen it?"

He captured her face between his hands, caressed her cheeks with his thumbs, and studied her gravely. He felt so much, so much more than he used to. What beat like a wild bird inside her. What burgeoned inside him. A demand for both claiming and release.

"I can't think of anything I'd like more."

Chapter Seventeen

In the fragile moments before she opened her eyes, Maj couldn't remember where she was. During the twenty-three years of her life, she'd awakened in a variety of places. Shop doorways. Deserted—except for her—back alleys. Even disgusting flophouses a few times. Most had felt wrong and she'd awakened on edge.

Not this time. This time, even before she opened her eyes, she knew that though she couldn't instantly recognize the place, she was where she was meant to be.

In a bed. And warm. Someone had his arms wrapped around her. Not just *someone* but the one person with whom she needed to be.

Benjamin. Oh, sweet heaven, she hoped it was early enough that she could make love to him again.

Making love to Benjamin felt like breathing. Necessary for life. It felt like eating good food after a long fast. No, better than all that.

She opened her eyes and saw where she was. The attic apartment on Congress. The bedroom was small, just large enough for the brass bed, a tiny bedside table, and a clothes rack. And it had only one window which now admitted dusty morning light.

Last night—they'd found sheets and blankets folded on the bottom of the mattress. She'd made up the bed while Ben explored the toilet which, as he said, was barely big enough for him to turn around.

Now he lay sleeping. She took advantage of that fact to examine him, letting her gaze roam at will. Neither of them wore a stitch of clothing, and he had his arms outside the blanket, clutching at her.

She liked what she saw. She liked his body a lot, from the brown hair on his arms to the interesting pattern that covered his chest and ran southward. She liked what lay down there even more.

Stubble had grown in on his jaw and it gave him a surprisingly rakish appearance. Maybe she was rubbing off on him.

She rolled over on top of him under the blankets. He had nice, long eyelashes as she was able to observe when they fluttered open, revealing those chocolate-brown eyes.

"Morning."

He groped visibly to place himself, even as she had. He ran the flats of his hands down her back and smoothed them along her skin.

"Umm. Morning."

"I love this place." She pressed up onto her elbows, the better to look at him. *I love you.* Only she couldn't say that. It would startle him too much, coming out of the blue like that, so quick, and him being a staid and steady sort.

But she did. She loved him on a terrifyingly intense level. She'd never ever felt this way about anyone.

"What time do you think it is? I need to get to work."

"Not yet, you don't. Anyway, it's Saturday."

"Is it?"

"Yes. Do you work on Saturday?"

"Not usually."

"We have two whole days. Here. Together."

With a magnificent sweep of lashes, his eyes opened wider and she saw herself reflected in them. Tiny. Shining brightly.

"Your eyes," she informed him, "are the color of chocolate. The first time I had chocolate was only a few months ago. Now I'm addicted. The first time I tasted it was—well, like the first time I kissed you. Now I'm addicted to you too."

He smiled lazily and she felt him. *Felt him*. His body of course, rising for her, and his spirit rising also.

She kissed his lips where they curved. One side and then the other.

"Umm," he said again. "Talk of chocolate makes me hungry. There's no food in the house."

"Good thing we have each other."

He buried his fingers in the wealth of her hair, which had come loose last night.

"I don't need anything else, Benjamin. Do you hear me? Nothing else but you."

"You sure about that?"

"Yes. I've never been so sure about anything."

****

When they surfaced again, it was snowing. Ben lay watching the big flakes splat against the window and wondered what had happened to his life.

Magenta sprawled with her head smashed against the middle of his chest, clutching him as if she'd never let go. Whether or not she slept, he couldn't tell.

She felt warm. She was warmth itself, soft and fiery and able to wring him out dry. To make him feel complete in a way he could barely contemplate, it was so bright.

He wondered if it was still Saturday. They needed to

get up, to go out and find something to eat.

They needed to make love again.

"Magenta?"

She didn't stir. Tired right out, then. Very gently he eased her off him onto the pillow and slid out of the bed.

Her hand came out and snagged his fingers. "Stay."

"I need the toilet."

She rolled over and regarded him. Bare-breasted, she looked wild with all that purple-red hair spread around her.

It was naturally black, as he could now attest, just like her eyes. How would she look with a black mop?

Beautiful. Perfect.

"I guess I can't argue with that."

He squeezed into the tiny washroom and looked at himself in the small, rectangular mirror hanging over the sink, blurry because he'd left his specs back beside the bed. He knew very well how he looked. Now, though—

He stared into the eyes of a stranger. Well, not a stranger, exactly. But that was not the mild, proper Benjamin Ambrose he normally presented to the world.

Magenta had changed him.

He splashed water over his face and went back out into the open area. The two attic windows showed him a world white from the river inward, as far as he could see. When he touched the glass, it made him shiver.

He ran for the bed.

"Here, let me warm you up."

She did a grand job of it, he had to hand her that. When he slid into her, she locked her heels behind his back. "Stay," she bade again. She pressed her lips against his cheek. "When you're inside me, I feel—"

"As you said, I don't think there are words."

"No. *Complete* comes close."

"Right. Whole, for the first time." He thought about it. "As if everything inside me is flowing in the right direction."

"Yes."

He kissed her again, slid his tongue into her mouth. Grew hard inside her.

They moved together, slowly at first. A wild dance. No longer two people but one.

"I'm starving," he confessed then.

"I suppose we could go out and get some food."

"It's snowing hard."

"I should go to Jamie Kilter's and fetch Pup. If we are staying here tonight." She sat up in the bed and turned her gaze on him. "Are we?"

Were they? What would his mother say? Two nights away.

"What's a Jamie Kilter?"

She laughed. "He runs the animal shelter down on Niagara Street. That's where I left Pup."

"All right. Is his name really Pup?"

"I guess I don't know yet."

They got up and dressed. The stairs stretched a long way down. Outside, the cold made Ben catch his breath.

White everywhere. Traffic—wagons and carriages—moved slowly and left deep ruts in the street. Most got stuck on the corners. Ben and Maj paused to help push out no fewer than three.

Part way down Niagara Street they saw a crowd of people gathered, an unusual sight in such weather.

"It's the start of the hockey tournament," Maj cried. "Look, the teams are arriving."

Among the milling people, it was hard to tell who

was who and what was what. But yes, there were groups of men—and a few women—in matching sweaters, some blue and some white, that must be the opposing teams. Buffalo's Best Brewing Company was just down the street. They'd built a rink here next to the river last year, when there'd been a tournament between Buffalo and Fort Erie, across the water in Canada.

This, if Ben understood it properly, was a contest between two teams formed of semi-professional players. There was a hockey school of sorts south of the city, headed by the controversial figure of Huritt Gilbert, the goalie who'd switched sides during that first tournament.

Ben saw him now, a big, rawboned fellow in a white sweater with a crop of black hair. He had at his side a redhaired woman who held a small child.

"There's Huritt Gilbert," Maj said, confirming it. "Come on, let's see if we can get his autograph."

She wanted the man's autograph? Should Ben be jealous? Instead he smiled.

Maj turned to him. "Everything's right—here, now. Can you feel it? Under the ground. We have to capture the moment."

He could feel it, so he followed her small, bright figure through the crowd till she reached the front.

Apparently all Huritt Gilbert's past sins had been forgotten. Howling fans mobbed him. The redhead must be his wife, and the child—who appeared the spit of him—could only be his son.

The rest of the team stood firm at his back.

"That's true," he was saying as they came up. "Nils Nilsson is heading the Steamies, the opposing team. Counting Nils himself, they have two hybrid automatons on their team. We—" he gestured to a hulking fellow in a white sweater, "have just one—Stanley, there."

"Shouldn't be allowed to play!" shouted someone from the rear of the crowd. "Ain't fair to have machines on the ice."

Those gathered turned on him—whoever he was, because Benjamin couldn't see—and shouted him down. Benjamin was pretty sure somebody also hit him with a hockey stick.

A news reporter stepped forward. "Mr. Gilbert, do you think the snow is going to hamper the games?"

"We hope not. We have a squad of steamies to keep the ice shoveled off. Of course, if this blizzard everybody's talking about arrives, all bets are off."

"Let's hope not. Do you know newspapers all over the country are calling Buffalo 'Snow City'?"

Gilbert's dark eyes flashed. "They don't know what Buffalo is, what it's made of. Sure, we have our snow, and our differences. But when the chips are down we're tough enough to endure both. We come together in the end, don't we?"

The crowd cheered. "Buf-fa-lo! Buf-fa-lo!"

"Mr. Gilbert!" From somewhere Maj had produced a slip of paper and a pencil. "Can I have your autograph?"

He smiled at her. So did the redheaded woman. "Sure."

He produced a scrawl which he thrust back at Maj. The flood gates opened. Everybody wanted autographs.

Maj wiggled her way out of the mob. Ben put his arm around her.

"I didn't know you liked hockey so much."

"Oh, yes. I used to sneak down when they were practicing on the river, to watch. I couldn't afford to get into any of the games. Oh look, there are food booths. Let's grab something before we go get our dog."

Our dog. Ben liked the sound of that.

Chapter Eighteen

"You'd better prepare yourself for your first sight of Jamie Kilter. Half his face is disfigured. It's quite shocking." Maj paused to catch her breath on yet another snow-clogged street corner. "But he's ever so kind."

She had tucked Huritt Gilbert's autograph away carefully in one of her many coat pockets, scarcely able to believe she'd got it.

Benjamin raised his eyebrows at her. "Should I be concerned? Are there rivals for your affection?" he teased.

She laughed and it felt good. "No—you have no rivals, Benjamin." She met his gaze and went weak in the knees. "Absolutely none."

"Good." He lifted her by the elbows and hoisted her over a snowbank.

"Besides, Jamie and Gilbert both have wives who adore them." Just like I adore you. She didn't add that. Not yet.

She had some kind of picture in her mind. They'd get Pup and go back to their new flat, which already felt like a refuge, settle in there with the cold and snow outside and all the warmth they created for each other within. And then she'd tell him.

For the first time within memory, all would be right with her world.

"Come on. It's just up ahead."

Jamie Kilter was otherwise engaged when they arrived, dealing with a man who'd apparently brought in a large and clearly underfed dog. The two of them were standing out on the front steps and visibly working up toward an argument.

"I can see you haven't been feeding him well. And in this condition," Jamie half shouted as they came up, "you can't put him to a pull-cart. Are you surprised he stumbled and went down?"

The man's face was mottled with red. "I feed him what I can. And I sure can't afford to take him to no animal doctor. Will you take him, or not?"

Jamie's wife, Cat, leaned out the door and signaled to Maj and Benjamin. Maj edged around the angry men, with Ben in tow, and went inside.

Every time Maj saw Cat Kilter, she was struck again by how very beautiful she was, even dressed in a plain skirt and blouse and with a little boy clutching her skirts.

"Come on in. Have you come for your wee dog?"

"Yes." Maj glanced over her shoulder. "Are they all right? Won't come to blows, will they?"

"Not so long as Jamie doesn't go off kilter."

The little family had quarters here, alongside the shelter. Barking came from out back, and a variety of animals wandered about.

Including Pup. He came running to Maj and put his front paws up against her knee.

"Hello, Darling." She picked him up.

"He's ever so sweet," Cat said. "I wouldn't mind keeping him. But," she looked around with a laugh, "it's not as if we have a shortage of others."

Jamie came in, face still like a thundercloud, and leading the enormous dog. His expression brightened when he saw Pup in Maj's arms.

"Oh, good, you've come back for him."

"Yes. Thanks so much." Maj nodded at the large dog, which appeared downtrodden. "I see you took him in."

"That idiot. Says he fed him when he could. I couldn't leave the beast in his hands."

"What worries me," Cat said, "is if we get this blizzard they're predicting there will be so many animals out there just trying to survive."

Ben dug in his pocket for some money. "Here, please take this for your expenses."

"And thank you for looking after Pup."

Jamie laughed. "You can't keep calling him Pup, can you?"

"I suppose not."

Outside on the street, the snow had eased up. But here, so close to the river, the wind cut like a blade. Maj shivered and Pup burrowed into her arms.

Ben shrugged his collar up higher around his ears. "Where to now?"

"I have to pick up my belongings from the Haven. I don't have much. I must tell you," Maj looked up at him, "I'm not very good with money and spend all I earn. I'll be better, I promise." She didn't want him to regret anything.

"I suppose I should collect a few things from my house, also."

"What will your mother say?"

"I scarce know." He took both her and the dog into his arms. They stood there with the big flakes of snow swirling down lazily, gazing into one another's eyes. "I scarce care."

Frightening. And astonishing, the way they both felt the strength of this thing between them.

"I'd best take Pup home first. Then maybe we should split up to collect our things."

He smiled. "Home. I like the sound of that."

****

"So you're back, then. Did you drop Winston off at the repair shop?" Mother stood in the doorway of the parlor, relief stark in her eyes. "Where's that—girl?"

"Magenta."

Mother made a face. "Wherever did you find her? A person like that."

"A person like what?"

"Well, you have only to look at her—"

"We've leased an apartment together on Congress Street."

"What! Congress Street? Benjamin, what are you thinking?"

"It's a decent neighborhood."

"That's not the point. This is not like you."

"You're right, it's not." Ben took off his hat. "Maybe that's the problem."

"The problem is you have some sort of disorder that causes you to die with very little warning. What if it happens when you're with—with her?"

"As a matter of fact, Magenta was recommended to help me with my spiritual ailment. That's what she's convinced is causing my—er—difficulties."

"She's no doubt a shyster! You mark my words."

A former thief, maybe, but not a shyster.

"Have you given her any money?" Reading Ben's expression, Mother cried, "Ben!"

"Mother, I don't want us to fall out over this. I'll be

126

staying with Magenta for the foreseeable future. I just came to collect some things."

"What about your job?"

"I'll still go to work. Nothing will change." He fixed her with a stern eye. "I just won't be living here."

Her mouth fell open and she touched a hand to her chest. "I think I'm the one who's dying."

He relented and went to her. "I don't want to upset you, Mother. But I am doing this."

"What if you do have a—an episode?"

"Then Magenta will help me." He kissed his mother's cheek. "You must have known I'd move out eventually and begin a life of my own."

"Not with—" She shut her lips abruptly. "I won't say it. You're clearly enamored with the woman, though to be utterly truthful I don't see why."

"Don't let the gaudy clothing fool you. Under it all, she's exactly what I need."

"I don't know what to say."

"Look, I'll talk to Lionel Pike, who's mending Winston. He fixes up secondhand steamies. Maybe he can send one over to help Dora keep the walks clear of snow and shovel your coal. I'm not deserting you, Mother. I'll just be gone for a while."

****

Maj reached the apartment first and climbed the many stairs with Pup—who'd refused to be parted from her—in her arms, then had to go back for her belongings, which she'd left in the downstairs hall. Maybe, she reflected on her way back up, a top floor set of rooms wasn't the best choice for a man who had a propensity for dying.

What if there was something wrong with his heart?

No, he'd said the physicians had pronounced him as healthy as a horse. Anyway, she'd listened to the steady beat of his heart all last night. And she knew very well his ailment was a spiritual one, somehow linked to the energies Maj could sense all around her, and beneath the ground.

She was what he needed. And he—oh, she'd never before admitted to needing anyone or anything. Not a man, of all things.

She stowed away the food she'd picked up at a shop on Grant Street and distributed her few possessions around the place. Then, with Pup in her arms, she knelt on the plank seat that fronted one of the windows and pressed her nose to the glass.

What if he didn't come? What if, away from her, free of the magical madness that had possessed them, he thought better of it? What if his mother dissuaded him? They were very close.

Cold came through the window. The snow had mostly stopped, but it grew dark in the streets below. Traffic had fallen off and figures—men or automatons, she couldn't tell which—shoveled the walkways.

Funny, all the fuss that had gripped the city over whether the automatons were here to help or harm, all the arguments and battles, and from up here she couldn't even tell them apart.

She sometimes thought people were born wanting to judge each other. Who's different from me, who's better, who's richer or poorer.

She'd been judged all her life. First, the guttersnipe with the runny nose and skinned knees, being raised by a cadre of thieves. Until she'd met Topaz, she hadn't known what a gypsy was, or why her hair and eyes were black, and her skin golden. Some people had thrown the word "mongrel" at her like it was an epithet. It wasn't. She'd known other individuals who bore that label and found them warm, kind, and generous.

Now, now she would be judged again—for the first time by somebody that mattered. If Benjamin found her wanting, if he never came back—

Suddenly she couldn't breathe. Need, raw and desperate, filled her chest to the brim. Below she couldn't see anyone walking. Just a steamcab sliding in the snowy street and a horse drawn cab—

The steamcab stopped in front of the house. When she saw the man climb out, she breathed again.

Chapter Nineteen

"I was afraid you wouldn't come back."

Benjamin turned in surprise when Maj spoke from the window seat. A single lamp burned in the room, in addition to the fire for which their landlord had provided coal. The place felt warm after the cold wind outside, and almost unbearably cozy.

"Why would you suppose that?"

"I thought if you got some distance from—from us, you might think better of it."

He looked at her, wondering what to say. His heart knelt there on the window seat. That scared him more than a little.

"Then I thought—thought taking rooms up at the top of the house was crazy, for a man who has episodes." She added in a whisper, "I'm sorry."

He dumped his possessions on the floor just inside the door and went to her. The small, scruffy dog frolicked around his feet.

He took Maj's face between his hands and looked into her eyes. "I wouldn't be anywhere else. All right?" He kissed her, hoping to say everything he couldn't with words.

She wrapped herself around him, arms and legs clutching his shoulders and hips. The stress flowed out of him to be replaced with that same sense of rightness.

He repeated it, when the kiss ended and she pressed

her face into his coat. "I wouldn't be anywhere else. Just with you. Here in this apartment. In this city."

"Yes?"

"Yes. With—with the snow and everything."

She gave a little sigh that sounded of contentment. "Are you hungry? I stopped and got food."

"I'm hungry for just one thing." And he carried her into the other room.

****

Time went away. Benjamin had never experienced anything like it. Outside, perhaps it snowed. Perhaps it didn't. The wind came in off the lake, down the long chute of the frozen black water, and rocked the tall house slightly.

Ben was where he needed to be. Where, in some curious heretofore-unseen fashion, he'd always been meant to be.

In this city. In this bed. In this woman's arms.

In the dark, he could feel her, really feel her. Not just the warm satin of her skin or the softness of her breasts or her slick heat, but what flowed through her. It didn't depend on the color of her hair or eyes, though he liked both those. What held him was that which animated her, and called to him.

It was best—strongest—when they were joined above and below. Then his heart beat strongest and he felt like the first man with the first woman.

They slept and woke and moved together again, rocking like the house. At some point, Maj got up, dressed, and took Pup out, brought him back, and fed him. After that they all three slept in the bed.

When he woke again, it was to the delectable smell of freshly made toast. He pried his eyes open one by one in time to see Maj crawling onto the bed with a plate in her hands, very nearly tipping it as she moved.

"What's that?"

"Toast. Are you hungry?" Her black eyes danced. "For food, I mean. I'm starving."

He pushed himself up against the pillows. Pale daylight filtered through the window. "You intend to eat that here in bed?"

"Why not?"

"I'm naked."

She grinned. "All the better. Here. I put on lots of butter, just the way I like it."

He accepted a crisp triangle. Bit into it with keen enjoyment

"I could live in this bed," Maj confessed. "So long as you're here."

"We'd soon run out of money."

"Aren't you the practical one? Anyway we'll worry about that on Monday. Today's only Sunday."

She wore an incredible garment—a robe, Ben supposed it would be called—sewn together from patches of every color. So only one of them was eating naked.

"You're spilling crumbs in the bed," he informed her.

"Does that bother you, my staid and proper fellow?"

"Not particularly. Just thought I'd point it out."

She paused with her toast halfway to her mouth. "Can you believe this? That we found each other, I mean."

"That it's…like this."

"This?" She crooked a brow.

"So perfect."

"Yeah, I know. It makes me go breathless every time I think about it. When I didn't know if you'd return last night—I couldn't breathe."

Pup jumped up on the bed, quite a feat for an animal with decidedly short legs, and begged a corner of toast.

"Do you plan to keep calling him Pup?"

Maj considered. "I don't suppose that's fair. Too much like when people used to call me Brat."

"People called you Brat?"

"Oh, yeah, all the time. Much worse, if I'm honest. Imp. Dirty thief. Little bastard. Of course," she reflected, "that last one's no doubt true."

"Is it?"

"Who can say? I never knew either of my parents. I figure they must have been thieves, because the first thing I remember is living with a whole bunch of people who did just that for a living. They more or less brought me up among them."

When Ben said nothing, she eyed him. "Does that make you sorry, Benjamin Ambrose?"

"Well, sure. It sounds like a rough beginning."

"What I mean is, are you sorry you got mixed up with—a woman like me?"

He caught her fingers, slick with melted butter, and brought them to his lips. "Not if she's you."

"Oh God, oh God." She leaned forward to kiss him and the plate tipped. Crumbs went everywhere.

"Come here, imp," he said, torn between fondness and passion.

Later they got up and dressed, and took Pup outside again. They encountered their landlord vigorously attacking the walk with a shovel.

"Good afternoon," he greeted them.

"Good afternoon, Mr. Riley," Maj returned.

"I trust you are finding the accommodations to your liking."

"They're wonderful, Mr. Riley. Just what we wanted."

"I am very glad."

"It snowed again," Ben contributed to the conversation, eyeing the levels of ever-rising snowbanks with some alarm.

"That is all it does, so it seems," replied Michael Riley, rather whimsically for a hybrid automaton. "If you stand and listen," he cocked his head, "you can hear the scraping of shovels for blocks and blocks."

"Any news of the approaching blizzard?" Maj asked.

"It is still approaching, according to the weather wizards," he told them. "If you will excuse me, I must get back to work."

They slipped off with Pup, Maj swinging Ben's hand.

"Maybe the blizzard will come roaring in right off the lake," she said, "and you and I will be snowed in together upstairs." She beamed at him. "Can you think of anything better?"

Offhand, Ben couldn't.

Chapter Twenty

"Good morning, Mr. Carter," Ben called through Mitch's office door on Monday morning. The small room where he worked was out back, along with a larger room where Mitch's boys—most of whom Mitch had known since they were all in the orphanage together—met.

Mitch glanced up at him and froze. He always dressed well, in good quality suits, but there remained something rough and dangerous about the man.

Mother had warned Ben off the job before he'd come to work here. Mitch Carter, though he did plenty of good in the city, had a reputation. He did business in sometimes brutal ways, had men beat up. Killed.

Ben hadn't listened, and Mitch had been good to him. Firm but fair. Just like when Mother warned him off Magenta, he thought now.

The sharp hazel eyes assessed him. "What's come over you, Ambrose?"

"Sorry?"

"You look different. You all right?"

Pinned in the doorway by that stare, Ben considered it. "I'm grand. Just grand." It had been a wrench parting from Maj this morning, after two solid days and nights in her arms. But he found he carried part of her with him.

"Maybe that's it. You look," Mitch searched for a word, "happy."

"Yes, sir."

"You'll have to be careful." One corner of Mitch's mouth curled up. "My other employees specialize in gloom and misery. Care to share the cause of your joy?"

"I've, er, met someone."

"Ah, I see. Is it the young lady who turned up here the other day? Nice girl, is she?"

Nice wasn't the word for Maj. Ben grinned. "She's amazing. Bright and funny and impulsive and everything I'm not."

Mitch gave a nod. "Come in here a minute. Do you think your girl—what's her name?"

"Magenta."

Mitch's brows rose. "Do you think Magenta would like to attend this hockey tournament everybody's talking about?"

"She'd be over the moon. She's a fan of Gilbert, the goalie."

"I have some tickets here that someone gave me." Mitch searched through the litter on his desk, located a bunch of tickets, and selected two." Here you go."

"Sir, thank you very much. I could never afford—"

"I should think not."

"I can't wait to tell her." So many long hours till he saw Maj again.

"Well, you're doing good work for us. I wanted to let you know that, following up on your report, I'm putting in an offer with the owner of Lost Waifs, to buy."

"That's wonderful news, sir. They'll be so happy."

Mitch nodded and waved a hand. "Off you go. Find me more orphanages. And you'd better pray tonight's game doesn't get cancelled for snow."

****

"Any more jobs come in, Magenta? I have no fewer

than three girls here anxious to fly the coop."

Topaz leaned in the doorway of the workroom. She looked magnificent, dressed in a long dusty-red skirt and a gold-colored overdress that had long, tight-fitted sleeves covered all over with embroidery, and a row of big brass buttons. Even her boots, high-heeled and black, looked splendid.

"All I've had come in this morning are demands for part-time workers, to shovel." Maj rifled through the slips of paper in her hand. She still had trouble reading quickly and her writing looked like something a child might produce, but Topaz didn't seem to mind.

"I thought the steamies were taking all those jobs."

"I guess there are people who refuse to employ steamies, even for shoveling, but still want their walks cleared."

Topaz frowned. "Will the rift in this city never heal? I thought things might get better after the hybrids came up with a cure for the plague last summer."

"It's been simmering," Maj informed her. "Beneath the surface." She could feel that.

"Well, let me know if something decent comes in."

"I will."

Topaz sauntered off, and Magenta thought about it. The division in the city went deep indeed, if there were still folks who, looking for cheap or transient help in a pinch, refused to hire an automaton.

She was lucky to have this job. Maybe she should go out and canvass for jobs, which she often did, her possessing a very persuasive tongue. If she saw a Help Wanted sign somewhere, she went in and often talked it into an opportunity for one of the girls. But it was so hard to get around the city right now. On her way in to work this morning, she'd had to climb over ruts up to her knees, and every second vehicle seemed to be stuck.

The whole city felt stuck, as a matter of fact.

Last night when they'd been lying in bed together all snug and warm, Benjamin had asked her about it.

"Tell me more about this energy you say runs beneath the city."

"There are lines of it, like rivers. Rivers of energy. Some are big and some are narrow, but they're meant to come together. And here, in Buffalo, they do—right beneath Niagara Square."

He'd been playing with her hair while he listened, curling a mahogany tress around his finger. Just to touch her. "I never heard of anything like that."

"And you had a good education, most likely." Unlike Maj. "It's not common knowledge. Just—I can feel it. For a long time I thought everyone could. But I asked around."

"Is there a name for these streams?"

"An old man I knew—his name was Dirk, and he was a thief—said they were called ley lines and that they're all over the world."

"And you think they're connected somehow to me?"

"Yeah." She'd gazed into his chocolate-brown eyes. Gone breathless once again. "I do. When all's well with them, you see—all's well with you. But sometimes they get blocked. By the bad emotions. Ugliness. Hate."

"And you think that's maybe when I—die?"

"I don't know. It's possible, isn't it?"

Now away from Ben, Maj didn't like to think of it. Because the city was in a bad way, folks angry on street corners and this monster blizzard poised to strike. What if something happened to Benjamin? Something dire, when she wasn't with him. It stole all her breath and, very nearly, her ability to think.

"Are you all right? Magenta?"

One of the girls, Kitty, stood by her desk.

"Only, you looked kind of queer just then. You sick?"

"No, I'm—I'm all right."

"Not going to pass out, are you? Do you have your monthly? I get all strange when I have mine."

"No, it's not that."

"I was thinking of goin' out after one of those shoveling jobs. I'm a big strapping girl, me, and extra money is extra money. What have you got?"

****

By four p.m. Maj felt desperate to see Benjamin. On her way home she marveled over it. Mere days ago she hadn't known he existed. Now she doubted she could exist without him.

They met in front of the tall, narrow house, and joy licked up in her so fierce she couldn't keep from grinning.

She seized his hands. "Benjamin."

He squeezed her fingers hard. "Magenta."

"Did you have a good day?"

"Yes, except for missing you. Say, how would you like to go to the hockey game tonight? Mitch gave me two tickets."

"I'd love it!"

"We'll have to take care of Pup and leave straightaway to get there in time. We can pick up something to eat outside the rink."

"I hope Pup hasn't made a mess while we were gone."

139

They found Pup curled up sleeping in one of the overstuffed chairs, took him out, and fed him. He seemed content to stay in out of the cold and snow after that.

The wind nearly took their heads off on the way to the rink down by the river. The place was already mobbed when they arrived, crowds of men standing about, gathered beside the massive Buffalo's Best Beer tent that had been set up.

They bought steaming meat pies at a stand, and a couple of beers to wash them down even though it seemed too cold for anything besides a hot beverage. The mood in the crowd, so Maj thought, was edgy, even incipiently ugly. Tough-looking men shouted slurs and insults at anyone wearing the opposing team's colors, and hollered insults at random passing automatons.

Just high game spirits, she told herself. But uneasiness lodged beneath her breastbone.

Their seats proved to be excellent ones. Halfway down the rink and nearly at ice level, they afforded a good view when the teams took to the rink.

The crowd, vocal from the start, greeted the players with cheers and jeers. The team in white were the Buffalo's Best Blades, led by Captain Huritt Gilbert, who got some cheers and also a few jeers due to him having changed sides during last year's tournament. He took his place in goal, his dark hair shining.

The hybrid players also took jeers, though with them out on the ice it was curiously hard to tell who was hybrid and who was human. The Steamers' captain, Nils Nilsson, himself a hybrid, just smiled at everyone indiscriminately as he swooped down the ice in practice, his fair hair flying.

Before the game started, Nilsson and Gilbert shook

hands cordially. Then all hell broke loose.

It was an ugly game from the start, not on the part of the players but on the part of the fanatics in the stands. They shouted, they cursed. They threw things onto the ice, some of which missed their distance and hit other members of the audience. That caused great ire and a few fist fights broke out. A man taking bets was pushed off the stands and had to be carried away by automaton medics.

Meanwhile, the first half of the match whizzed by in close contest. First, one of the hybrids scored for the Steamers, but Gilbert kept all the ensuing pucks out and the Blades scored twice in rapid succession.

By the break between halves, the arena had reached near-manic level. Crowded from both sides and behind, Ben looked at Maj. "Want to leave? It's getting pretty crazy in here."

"It is, isn't it?" She ducked as a metal object sailed past her head and crashed into the wooden boards that separated the rink from the stands. "I'd like to see the end of the game. I think the Blades are going to win, don't you? If Gilbert can hang on."

His eyes met hers. "Do you think it's safe? There are an awful lot of arguments going on." One had broken out just down the row from them that looked to come to blows.

"I don't know. There is a police presence."

"Yes, but they're throwing things at the police."

Throwing things seemed to be the order of the day. After some fans went out during the break to the food stalls, food joined the melee.

The police broke up the fight down the row after one punch had been thrown. Ben put his arm around Maj and tucked her in close.

"Can you feel it?" she asked into his ear. "The energy?"

He could. It seemed to pound right up in his chest. He thought they should leave. But she wanted to stay. If things turned truly nasty, he'd just have to protect her.

Another shouting match broke out behind them. "Damned automatons shouldn't be allowed in the game! They shouldn't even be allowed in the building. Hockey's a man's game. And how is allowing hybrids fair to the other players? I ask you that."

"It takes the game up a notch having the hybrids in. If you can beat one of them hybrids, you know you've done something!"

"So I s'pose you could outrun a steam engine, could you?"

"Not sayin' that. But the automatons are here to stay—"

"Not if we banish them all!"

"Tried that last summer, didn't we? Look what happened. They wound up saving our asses."

"They should all be decommissioned, including the hybrids."

"That's half the police force!"

"Who needs the god-damned Irish Squad?"

"They're the only ones keepin' order in this city. Maybe it's the humans who should go."

"You take that back, you—you dirty low-down metal lover!"

Ben and Maj looked at each other. And hell broke loose all over again.

Chapter Twenty-One

People came flying over the top of the seats, barely missing Maj and Ben where they sat, Maj within the circle of Ben's arm. Instinctively they both ducked, and he drew her into his lap as something heavy landed on them and slithered off.

Members of the crowd were screaming, hollering, and swearing. Whistles blew and the sound of blows landing, skin on skin, echoed from every side.

"We have to get out of here," Ben said.

He got up, doing his best to shelter Maj's body with his own, and began fighting his way out of the row. It wasn't easy. Men battered each other in front of them and behind. Ben pushed them out of the way, using his muscle, and Maj hung onto the front of his coat.

The energy around, within, and beneath her surged, angry now, ugly and dangerous.

They reached the aisle and began to pick their way down the wooden stairs. Fortunately they weren't many rows up. If they could only get out of the building—

It proved impossible. Down on ground level, chaos reigned. People ran by armed with what looked like tools, and right in front of them two men beat down one of the automatons that had been handing out fliers.

Ben edged ahead of Maj and tried to pull them off. One of them turned on him, and Maj with a wild cry drew him away. They ducked and wove, Maj now in the lead.

She could feel Ben behind her, sense his nearness.

And then she couldn't.

A brawl separated them—at least a dozen men struggling and wrestling together had come between. Punches were thrown, and Maj cried out. Fighting hard, pushing bodies for all she was worth, she turned back and tried to see Benjamin.

She couldn't.

No brown head, no broad shoulders. No chocolate-brown eyes searching for her. Worse, she couldn't *feel* him.

What did that mean?

Emotions surged within her, rage and terror. She pushed a man twice her size to get him out of her path and struggled back the way she had come.

No sight of Benjamin.

How could he just be gone? He'd been right behind her.

Bodies littered the ground, many being trampled. Someone on the ice—it sounded like Huritt Gilbert— shouted through a bullhorn, trying to call for order, maybe.

"Benjamin! Benjamin!" She screeched his name. No reply.

Someone shoved her and she staggered. At the same instant, she glimpsed a pair of legs to one side.

She knew those legs.

Unable to force her way past the men struggling behind her, she got to her knees and crawled through, receiving several hearty kicks in passing. When she reached Ben at last—and it was Ben, lying sprawled— two men stood punching each other just in front of him.

Surging to her feet, Maj pushed at one of them. "Let

me by!"

A big, ugly brute, he turned on her. "Shut up, girlie."

"Move. I need to reach my—"

He punched her. She ducked which spared her the worst of it, because he would have flattened her. His fist grazed her cheekbone and she drew her knife, the one she always carried in one pocket.

"Move or I'll stick you," she snarled.

He moved, and she fell to her knees again, beside Benjamin.

"Ben? Ben?"

Was he dead? Had the evil energy of this place affected him and brought on another episode?

But no. When she turned his face toward her she saw a great bloody wound on his left temple. He'd been hit.

"Oh God, oh God, please."

She gathered him up against her, there amid the pushing, the fighting, and the angry feet. His spectacles had fallen off his face and lay beside him on the floor, miraculously in one piece, so she snatched them up and crammed them into her pocket. She couldn't lift Ben— he was much too heavy for her. She needed help.

She closed her eyes and willed it. Willed it with all her might and everything in her being. *Help.*

And opened her eyes in time to see a pair of legs clad in blue run past her. She sprang up and threw herself at their owner.

A policeman.

"You have to help me!"

He looked at her. Tall and strapping, he had hair almost as red as her own, and bright green eyes. She knew him: Pat Kelly, who'd given her a list of rental properties owned by automatons.

"Miss Rask?"

"You have to help me, Officer Kelly. My—my lover. He's been knocked down. Over there."

"Your lover?"

"Yes. Please. He's hurt, and if we leave him there he'll be trampled."

Thanks to all that was holy, Kelly came with her, shoving his way through with his powerful shoulders, giving a push here and there accompanied by, "*Sor*, please."

When they reached Ben, Pat Kelly bent down and examined him. Then, without so much as a glance for Maj, he picked Ben up, a feat that could be accomplished only by a hybrid with superhuman strength.

"Miss Rask, stay close and follow me."

Carrying Ben the way another man might a child, he made his way out through the rampant chaos, Maj clutching the back of his coat.

Outside, ambulances—both horse-drawn and steam-powered—fought with the food stands for space. The fights had spilled over out here. Squads of policemen, Irish or otherwise, strove for control. The wind cut like a knife and blood splashed the snow.

Pat Kelly paused as if to get his bearings.

Maj appealed to him. "Is he alive? Alive?"

"Miss, I cannot tell. We need to get him to one of the ambulances."

He bulled his way—not to the nearest, which all appeared full—but to one standing at a distance.

"This man needs care," he told the medics, who had him carry Ben into the back of their vehicle.

Beneath the steam lamps, Ben looked even worse. He looked dead.

Maj seized Pat Kelly's arm. "Thank you."

"You are welcome, miss. I must get back."

"Yes, of course. Thank you!" She called it after him and clambered into the vehicle.

She found the two medics, one youthful and the other older, bent over Benjamin.

"Is he dead?"

"No, miss. He's not in a good way, though. You can see he was in the fight—his knuckles are split. And he's taken a blow to the side of the head, likely from a wrench or other metal implement."

"We need to take him to the hospital," said the younger man.

"Can I come with?"

They eyed her closely. "Are you his—wife?"

"Yes. Yes, I am." It might be the only way they'd let her come with them.

They nodded at each other. "All right. If we can get out of this tangle of traffic, we should be in business. Jesse, you go drive."

It wasn't until they were out on the street, battling both snow and other vehicles, that Maj realized Benjamin's mother should be contacted. The poor woman would be worried sick if she knew.

Maybe better then, if she didn't know, Maj decided. She perched on the edge of the cot and held Ben's hand while the ambulance slid and shuddered.

She, Maj, was here with him now. All he needed.

Chapter Twenty-Two

He seemed to be floating down a river, flat on his back and bobbing the way a small boat might. The river, though, wasn't composed of water so much as energy. He'd fallen somehow into one of Maj's underground streams.

Maj. Where was she?

He couldn't feel her, not the way he did when they lay in bed together, and yet in a curious way, she was part of the river where he floated.

"Maj?"

"I'm here. I'm here, my darling."

With the sound of her voice everything snapped back into place. He became aware of movement, and her hand clutched his tightly.

She was here. All right, then, whatever else happened.

She'd called him her darling. Well, of course she had. They were the two halves of one another, weren't they?

He tried to open his eyes so he could see her, and failed. He could see her anyway—deep black eyes, gamine face.

"I can't open my eyes."

"You were hit in the head. At the hockey game, remember? At least you're not dead. I don't know what I'd do if—"

The bobbing of his little boat ceased.

"We've arrived at the hospital, Benjamin."

Doors slammed. Ben was jostled and lifted, but Maj kept hold of his hand.

"Maj? What if I can't see again?"

"It's all right. I'll still be here."

"No matter what?"

"No matter what."

****

Maj paced the corridor while a harassed-looking physician treated Benjamin. She wondered, as she paced, what had happened to her. She'd worked pretty hard all her life to make sure she needed no one. She'd been on the outside, always. The strange child raised by thieves. The girl who never had to go to school and had no friends as such—at least not for long. Never for long. The people in her life came and went. Pseudo parents, guardians, companions.

She hadn't wanted a lover. Only, in some part of her being she must have, because she'd jumped for Benjamin like a starving wolf for a lamb.

And now here she was desperate and praying he would stay in her life.

"Miss?" The doctor called to her from inside the room.

"Yes?" She hurried in.

"You can take him home. We're mobbed here tonight and have no room for him."

"Is he all right? Can he see?" Her gaze flew to Benjamin where he sat half propped up on a gurney. Watching her in return.

Oh, thank God!

"You'll have to watch him carefully for signs of

concussion. I wouldn't let him fall asleep. If he gets groggy or can't speak clearly, call for help. Don't leave him alone."

"I certainly won't leave him. And I won't let him fall asleep."

The doctor squinted at Maj. "What about you, miss?"

"What about me?"

"Do you want to be treated before you leave? It looks like you have a shiner coming up."

"Oh. Somebody punched me. I'm fine. Only—how am I going to get him home?"

"I'm sure I don't know, miss. There are often cabs outside, but it's a busy night."

He dashed out, leaving Maj and Ben gazing at one another.

"I can walk home."

"No, you can't." She went to him, took his face between her hands, and kissed him. The tumultuous energy inside her settled a bit.

"Now I'm sure I can walk." He smiled at her. "Possibly on water."

"There's a push chair over there. I can at least push you to the door."

He touched her cheekbone gently. "You were punched."

She nodded. To her horror, tears came to her eyes. "I was so scared." She repeated it. "I thought I was going to lose you. Just when—just when I've found you."

"You won't."

"I—"

"Magenta, you won't lose me."

"You promise?" An impossible promise to give or

keep. Things happened in life. Things nobody could control.

But he said, "I promise."

She blinked the tears away. "Let's go, then. I just want to get you home. I hope there's a cab."

"I don't think I have money for a cab."

They struggled out through the main doors, Ben leaning on Maj more than was probably good for him. Outside, a miracle awaited them. A single cab stood in a lane along one side. The driver leaped out when they appeared and opened the door for them.

"Sir, ma'am. You look like the walking wounded. Been in that scuffle at the hockey game?"

"Yes, I'm afraid so."

"Word on the street is there are riots breaking out all over the city." The driver, a short man with a balding head, frowned. "Seems like the city's been a powder keg just waiting for a match."

"Yes."

"Go on, get in."

"I don't think I can afford the fare," Ben said unhappily.

"Where you headed?"

"Up on Congress."

"Tell you what, that's on my way home and I'm figuring on packing it in for the night. I'll drop you off on my way." He added when they exchanged glances, "No fee."

"That's very kind of you," Ben said.

"No matter. Looks like you've had a hard enough night."

The cab, steam-powered, slid and spun its tires most of the way home. Maj didn't mind.

Getting Ben all the way up those stairs was another matter. Their landlord did not appear to be home. Likely out striving to keep the peace.

Pup greeted them happily. As soon as Maj got Ben settled in one of the chairs, she ran the dog out and back again. She closed the door firmly and shot the bolt.

"We're not going anywhere," she announced.

"Work tomorrow."

"If the city's in riot, Mayor Piffin may shut everything down."

"I don't mind if he does."

"Are you in pain? Does your head ache?"

"A bit."

"Do you want me to run out and get some powders?"

"If you think I'd let you go out there for any reason—"

"But you need—"

"What I need is for you to come here."

She shed her coat and perched in his lap, cuddling close.

"I thought you'd died. When I saw you lying there…"

"So you said. Apparently I'm not that easy to finish off. At least, not permanently."

Maj wanted to tell him she loved him. She wanted it so much she ached. She didn't think he was ready to hear it.

She wound her fingers into the front of his shirt. "I could feel it, couldn't you? When all that fighting broke out, the anger and the disharmony. I could feel it in the energy beneath my feet."

"Disharmony—that's a good word for it. It's like a song that's supposed to play out, but it doesn't. Instead it gets balled up. Tangled."

"We're the song, you and me," she told him, and kissed him.

"Let's go to bed."

"Benjamin, I don't think we should. I'm supposed to watch over you."

"You can watch me real close, there."

"And keep you from falling asleep."

"You'd better keep me up, then."

But she wouldn't be tempted. Instead, gazing at him seriously, she said, "You should send a message to your mother. To tell her you're all right."

"Since she doesn't follow hockey, she won't know there's been a bruhaha."

"She'll find out if there's rioting in the city."

"Maj, I want you to look after me. Only you. I want this place to be our haven, our world. At least for a little while."

"I want that too."

"Then stay where you are."

She quieted with her head tucked against his chest.

"Your mind's like a little bird, isn't it?" He sounded amused. "Always fluttering."

"Sometimes in opposite directions," she admitted. Stealing a glance at him, she asked, "I suppose your thoughts are always quite orderly?"

"Usually." He appeared to think about it. "When I'm with you, they come into line."

"Same here."

They subsided into silence, watching snowflakes strike the window. Comfort, deep and wide, came stealing in.

Maj relived again, in her mind, that terrible moment

she'd seen Benjamin lying on the ground. She couldn't help but do. From the circle of his arms, though, it didn't look half so frightening.

She could save him, she vowed... No, they could save each other.

Chapter Twenty-Three

Magenta had very little sleep that night. She dozed off a few times but always pulled herself awake again, afraid if she slept, Ben would also.

At first light she tiptoed into the tiny washroom and peered at herself in the wavy mirror. Her entire left cheekbone and half her left eye had turned purple. It contrasted horrifically with her mahogany-colored hair.

Ben, as she decided when she tiptoed back and peered at him propped against the pillows, didn't look much better.

She dressed and took an eager Pup outside. It had snowed most of the night. She had to borrow the landlord's shovel from next to the front door and clear out a place for the diminutive dog to relieve himself. Then she walked down to the corner and bought a newspaper, which she took back and spread across the bed.

"Look at this."

Riots Cripple Buffalo, the headline screamed. *Multiple arrests at hockey tournament and throughout the city.*

She puzzled through the stories. Benjamin's eyesight still being blurry, and learned that the mayor had locked down the city due to a combination of snow and violence.

"Automatons were beaten and destroyed. Killed, if

you can call it that."

"I'm glad Winston's safe at Pike's."

"Yes, but there's an awful lot of other damage. It says windows were broken on any known automaton or hybrid-owned properties."

"Again? That's what they did last summer when they thought the hybrids had created the plague."

"'They?'"

"The people in the city who don't want automatons around. Why can't people just leave each other alone?"

"The age-old question."

"Seriously, where will it end?" Maj looked at him. "Do you feel all right?"

"Except for this big crack on the side of my head."

"Because when I went out I could feel how off everything is—the energy, that is. If you're tied to the city and that's what's been causing you to have episodes when you d-die—"

"I'm fine. So long as you're here with me."

"Still." She shivered. "Benjamin, it scares me."

"Sweetheart, I don't know how to make everybody get along." Ben tapped the newspaper spread across their knees. "Sounds like it would take something catastrophic."

"Well, at least with the city shut down, we don't have to worry about going to work."

"Always a silver lining."

****

When Ben shuffled his way into the tiny washroom and looked at himself in the mirror, he cringed. No wonder Maj was so worried about him. Good thing he had a hard head.

Maj came and leaned against the door, which for

purely claustrophobic reasons he'd left open.

"I'm a mess," he observed.

"As am I."

"Part of my hair's gone on this side."

"I think they shaved it, in the hospital, to get at the cracked skull."

"It certainly shows off the wound to best advantage."

"I think so." She smiled. "Makes you look rather dangerous."

"I'll have to get a message to Mother and make sure she's all right. It's a good thing she can't see me like this."

He washed his face and reached for his razor.

"Uh-uh!" Maj objected.

He raised an eyebrow at her.

"I like the beard."

"You do?"

"It adds to the general air of rakishness."

"I've never before been accused of rakishness."

"Things have apparently changed. Between the beard and the blood, you appear quite the adventurer."

"Do you want me to be an adventurer?" he asked uncertainly.

"I want you to be you." Mischief flared in her eyes. "Want me to prove it?" She squeezed into the room, shut the door and fell to her knees. "Some things, we don't want Pup to see."

Later they took the dog out together so Ben could get some air, and bumped into their landlord who, in company with a late-model automaton, once more shoveled the walk.

"Have you met your other neighbor?" Michael Riley

asked, indicating the automaton, who politely ceased working to look at them.

"This is Gamet. He and his wife have the floor down from you, as I have the ground floor."

"Wife?" Maj asked.

"Yes. My partner is also an automaton." Gamet added proudly, "We were married in the new Steam Church."

"Pleased to meet you." Ben extended his hand.

"My wife, Maybell, went out to work at the laundry. Her employer demanded all the non-humans report to work despite the mayor's edict. I will walk down soon and meet her, to escort her safe home. There have been so many terrible attacks."

Michael Riley tapped the unit on what passed for a shoulder. "I'll go with ye, Gamet. Just to make sure all's well."

Riley turned to Benjamin. "Have you had an accident, *sor*?"

"No, we were at the hockey game last night."

"Ah, that would explain it."

"What do you think about the chances of this blizzard that's supposed to be coming?" Maj asked Riley. "Do you think it will strike?"

Riley gazed away toward the river as if scenting the wind, which of course he couldn't actually do. "Who can say, miss? Buffalo has already been labeled by the national papers as Snow City."

"Better that, perhaps," Gamet suggested, "than for the newspapers to focus on our unrest." He turned to Maj and Benjamin. "Welcome to the building. I hope you will be very happy here."

"Nice fellow," Ben remarked as they walked away

and only later realized what he'd said.

Battered and determined to keep one another warm, they slept away much of the afternoon—Maj figuring it must be safe for Benjamin by now—and awoke for another Pup outing and meals all round. They returned to bed for the night, only to awake to another day of city-wide shutdown.

The mayor had put out a statement carried in that morning's *Courier Express*—Riley let them borrow his copy—saying for the safety of the city, he banned unnecessary travel.

Sectors of the city are not all safe, he said. *The blizzard is still predicted to strike. I suggest everyone procure a six-pack of Buffalo's Best Beer from the nearest shop, and then stay at home.*

Citizens seemed less willing to cooperate with that advice today, however. Drays and delivery wagons rumbled by down the street. The city had to be supplied and, as Maj said, even if people obeyed the mayor's edict, the beer had to be distributed somehow.

Ben didn't know what to do. Feeling restless, he decided to walk down to Pike's Steam Repair and see if Winston was ready.

Pike and his crew were hard at work, in defiance of the shutdown.

"Your unit's not ready quite yet," Lionel Pike told Ben. "We're trying to get some parts of the right vintage, and as you can imagine, it's not easy with the city shut down."

"I can imagine."

"What happened to your head, if I might ask?"

"Hockey game."

Dammit began to chortle. "You were there, sir? It

sounds like it was quite the melee."

"I'm lucky I got out alive. The city's just—well, all stirred up."

Dammit offered, "I've been out patrolling the last two nights, trying to make sure no other automatons get battered. Some of us are quite defenseless."

"I see."

"There is talk of forming an all-metal volunteer army to try and patrol regular."

"I don't think that would be wise," Ben offered his opinion. "Won't it just aggravate the metal-haters and make them more aggressive?"

"That's what I told him," Pike put in.

"Anyway, isn't that the police's job?"

"Yes, sir. But the police can't be everywhere. We can."

Leonard Pike's gray eyes met Ben's for an instant. *Something bad's brewing*, they seemed to say.

"I hope the residents of the city can all find a way to work together. Mr. Pike, I was going to ask you another favor. You've been sending rebuilt units to help at the orphanages and hospitals, haven't you? I wondered if you might have a second-hand unit I could purchase to send to my mother's home. Now that I've moved out, she will need help with simple maintenance and snow-clearing. Once Winston's repaired, I'll want him with me. I'm afraid I couldn't pay much—"

Lionel glanced at his aged unit. "Mordred, is Roland ready?"

"Almost, Master Lionel. I just have to get the rest of the rust off him and polish his skin."

"Let's send him out on assignment. Mr. Ambrose, I have a unit here—Roland—we just finished overhauling.

He's old."

Mordred put in, "Probably even older than me."

"Probably," Pike agreed. "But he's desperate to be of use. He may still have a few quirks to work out, but I'd be willing to send him to your mother on trial. If she likes him, and if"—Pike held up a finger—"he likes it there, you could pay me later."

Mordred again interjected, "We never send any of our units where they do not want to go."

"So I'll have to ask him, of course. If he's willing for the trial, I can have Dammit drop him off. Just give him your mother's address."

A new world, Benjamin thought, or at least a new Buffalo, where steam had a choice.

Gravely, he said, "I would be most grateful for that. As for when I can pay—"

Pike gave him a level look. "Don't worry about it. This project is backed and largely funded by Miss Ginny Landry. Do you know her?"

"I think I saw her at a tavern a few nights back. If it's the lady I'm thinking of."

"Brown hair, cowboy boots, and a fringed coat? Often wears a clever little steam cannon. She cares a lot about the fate of older steam units."

"Ah." It had definitely been Ginny Landry, then, at the Rabid Rabbit that first night he and Maj had— "I've seen her. She travels in company with a big Irish policeman?"

"Yes, Brendan Fagan, Captain in the Buffalo Police Force."

Mordred lowered his voice to a sonorous level. "She's his lady. No use any other man looking her way."

"No worries. I've got all I can handle in that

department."

"Me too." Lionel grinned for the first time, and it warmed his face, making him look younger. "Just as Dammit has his Verna and Mordred, here, his beloved Wendy. We're all happy men. Now we just have to figure out a way to get the city in line."

Chapter Twenty-Four

From the high sitting room windows, whenever it stopped snowing, Magenta could just glimpse the river. From this distance it looked like a dark ribbon of steel. Beyond it, as she knew, stretched Lake Erie, all frozen over and at the moment covered with a thick layer of snow.

The long expanse of the lake seemed to hang in Maj's consciousness while she tried to do other things. Straightened the rooms and made the bed. Put some more of her belongings away. Paid attention to Pup and prepared a simple meal for when Benjamin returned.

Benjamin. He too hung in her consciousness, a tangible presence.

This was the first time she'd been apart from him since the riot at the hockey game. She hadn't wanted to let him go out on his own and had to fight down her protective impulses. Because Benjamin was a grown man and presumably able to look after himself. But he wasn't just any man. He was the man she loved. One with a propensity for dying.

She paced the floor and spoke to Pup as she waited. "I shouldn't have let him go alone. It's so dangerous out there right now. On the other hand, I don't want to smother him, do I?"

Pup gazed at her uncertainly and wagged his stubby tail.

"Maybe if I try to explain to him how important he is to me, if I tell him I love him—"

That stopped her cold. She had never in her life told anyone she loved them. She wasn't sure she had ever loved anyone before now. Oh, she'd become attached to those around her, the people who'd helped to bring her up in their rough fashion. But those people all seemed to disappear eventually.

Was that why she was so afraid of losing Benjamin? Because this, what she felt, just wasn't natural.

He felt like part of her, as no one else ever had. Yet if he were part of her, and such a vital part, how could she have lived the past twenty-three years without him?

Anyway, it was risky caring so much for anybody. Especially in this dangerous world.

She heard footsteps on the stairs, coming up. Her heart leaped alarmingly and she held her breath till he reached the landing. She threw the door open.

Oh, he looked good. Well, he still looked a bit of a mess, with some of his hair shaved off and a bandage on the side of his head, but he looked good anyway, in a manner she couldn't begin to define.

Pup frolicked at his feet, and he bent to pet the animal affectionately.

"No Winston?" she asked.

"He isn't ready yet. I've made arrangements to—"

He paused when Magenta flew into his arms, wrapped her arms around him, and squeezed tight. She burrowed into him.

"Ah. Ah, darling." He enfolded her and drew her still closer. They stood that way for a while, Maj couldn't tell how long, while once again the pieces of her world fell into place.

"Please don't leave me anymore."

"I think I'll have to. I'm pretty sure we'll both have to go to work tomorrow."

"I don't like it."

"Now, where's the spunky girl I first met? You're the strong one who can face anything."

"Except being apart from you."

His arms tightened. She felt his lips in her hair and tipped up her head. She searched his face, touching every feature before she said, "You called me 'darling.' "

"That's what you are, isn't it? My little, feisty darling."

Maj couldn't remember anyone ever calling her by a pet name. Except, as she'd confessed, Brat.

"Does your darling warrant a kiss?"

It started out slowly, gently, his lips cold on hers, and grew steadily warmer. Comfort came stealing in. What matter if the world outside blew apart? So long as they were together here.

"I made us something to eat."

"It smells good."

"Take off your coat and sit down."

They conversed as they ate, Benjamin telling her about the state of *Out There*, all he'd seen and what the crew at Pike's had said. When he finished, Ben laid aside his knife and folk and regarded Maj seriously.

"I wanted to ask you about these lines of energy you can feel running beneath the city."

She nodded. "You can feel them too."

"Sometimes. Not, I think, as clearly as you can." His chocolate-brown eyes studied her. "You say they become disrupted from time to time?"

"Yes."

"And you think those times coincide with the unrest in the city. Answer me this: Are the disruptions the cause of the unrest? Or does the unrest prompt the disruptions?"

"That's a good question. I'm not sure it's possible to tell." She leaned her chin on her hand, elbow on the table. "Just, as a spiritualist—that's what Topaz insists I am, and since she's one too and I figure she must know—I can feel there's a strong force running beneath the city."

"Corresponding with parts of it."

"Yes."

"And you believe, corresponding also with me? So when it becomes especially erratic, I have an episode, and die?"

Maj did not like talking about that. But yes, she was supposed to be helping him. It was the reason they'd come together.

"Yes."

"Why me? Why me, Maj? Out of a whole city full of people, why would I be connected to this—this force? I'm the most boring, ordinary—"

"You're not."

"I really am, you know."

"You're anchored here somehow. I don't understand it, but it's so. You're like the bedrock, the stone beneath the lake. Beneath the land."

He didn't say that sounded mad, but she thought she caught a glimpse of it in his eyes.

"All right. So how do we cure that? Cure me from dying?"

"By healing the city, maybe."

"We—you and me—are supposed to heal the city? When people can't get along at a hockey game?"

"I know it sounds mad. We were barely surviving without each other. But, Ben, together, we're stronger."

"Not all that strong. Look at the state of everything. Humans hating automatons despite what they did for us last summer. Automatons talking about forming a metal army to protect themselves. Unrest on every corner. Riots, windows getting smashed. And now this big blizzard coming."

"It seems like a lot to overcome, I know." She reached across the table to capture his hand. "How do we possibly fix all that? By believing, I think. That has to be the secret to it. Yes, there's discord, but there are also people and automatons all over the city who are doing good. I work for one of them. So do you, with the improvements at the orphanages. Look at Jamie Kilter."

"And Lionel Pike," Ben had to agree. "He's helping the old units he sets up and also the places where he and Ginny Landry send them."

"What do they all have in common?" Maj's gaze held his. "They believe in what they're doing. They believe that the good can outweigh the hate in this city, and set all the energies right."

No sooner had she spoken the words than a tremendous crash resounded from below. Maj jumped violently and Pup gave a little, sharp bark. They all leaped up.

"What was that?" Maj gasped.

"I don't know, but—"

A second crash interrupted Ben and then a third.

"That came from downstairs." Ben told Maj, "Stay here. Keep Pup in. I'll go see."

"If you think I'm letting you go without me—"

"Just keep Pup safe." Before she could protest further, he ran out. Without his coat.

Chapter Twenty-Five

Though she hated to do it, Maj shut Pup into the bathroom before she grabbed her coat and Ben's and followed him down the stairs. She went so quickly she stumbled on the narrow steps and almost fell.

She ran into Ben, quite literally, when she crashed into his back at the outer door where he stood peering through the gaping hole that used to be a glass window.

He gave her an exasperated look but didn't protest her presence.

"What happened?"

"Somebody threw a rock through the glass, and the other downstairs front windows. Riley's not home—neither's his wife. I pounded on their door. He must be out keeping the peace."

An irony, Maj thought.

He started to open the door. She seized his arm. "Don't go out. They could still be there."

"Gamet's gone out. I have to help."

He flung the door open. Maj could see Gamet then, standing halfway down the walk, shouting at someone and waving his arms.

Even as Ben ran out, another rock came sailing from a group centered in the street. Men—or women—all muffled against the cold. Aimed not at the house this time but at Gamet, the missile struck the unit in the head and rocked him.

About to summon Ben back again, Maj caught herself. What had they just been talking about upstairs? That helping each other was a form of healing. How could she call him back?

Instead she ran out behind him, even as he placed himself between the unit and the crowd of marauders. "What are you doing?" he called. "Leave him alone. He's not bothering you!"

"He's a God-damned automaton. Nothing harmless about any of 'em. This house belongs to an automaton too—one of them hybrids."

"We're taking things into our own hands," yelled another man. "So get out of the way."

"I won't!" Ben stood there foursquare, his head bandaged and without his coat, unarmed. And, Maj thought, he called himself ordinary.

She shrugged into her coat—her knife being in the pocket—before running forward with Ben's coat, which she flung over his shoulders. A little padding, if more missiles started flying.

"Maj," Ben said, "help Gamet inside, will you?"

She'd rather stand shoulder to shoulder with him. But another rock sailed in, missing Ben but striking Gamet once more with a resounding clang. She ducked back, grabbed the unit by the arm, and tried to pivot him.

"You live here?" Another voice called. "Your landlord's a member of the Irish Squad. Did you know that? They're the worst of the lot—buying up properties, building churches—churches, of all things!—and even manufacturing more monstrosities like themselves."

"They're making hybrid children! From corpses. It's an unholy travesty."

"We're gonna show them they're unwelcome in this

city. Pay visits to their properties, that should belong to people like us."

Maj, with Gamet in tow, had reached the steps when the next rock came flying. She heard the thump when it hit Benjamin in the shoulder. Not unlike Gamet, he swayed but did not go down.

Abandoning Gamet, Maj ran back to him. She put her body in front of his and spread her arms. "I have a knife and I swear I'll cut the next person who throws a rock."

They laughed at her and sniggered. Ben caught her from behind, his hands on her upper arms, to move her aside.

"Go inside, Maj."

"I want—"

"I'm all right."

At that moment, a phalanx of policemen appeared, charging down the street two abreast with a lone uniform out in front. They stepped in unison, their boots hitting the slush underfoot with a sound like the hooves of horses.

The vandals scattered. Most of them took off straight up Congress. Some ran into opposing yards, one man—nothing more than an anonymous, bundled form—scaling a snowbank to get away.

The phalanx of hybrid policemen went in pursuit.

"Let's get him inside," Ben said and, supporting Gamet between them, they humped him up the steps and struggled into the hallway and even more laboriously to the second floor.

A steam unit stood on the landing, peering down. This must be Maybell, Maj thought. Gamet's wife of whom he'd spoken when they first met.

A diminutive unit, she had a highly polished head with dished features—common among utilitarian automatons—and scarred, worn hands. As much as it could be said of a mechanical, she looked worried.

"Bring him in, please. Bring him in. Is he damaged?"

"I'm not sure," Ben told the unit.

The interior of the flat felt cold. It took Maj an instant to grasp that this was because both front-facing windows had been shattered. A number of rocks lay on the floor along with a litter of glass shards. Icy air, and ice-laden snow, blew in.

The apartment itself looked rather barren, the way the attic had when Maj and Ben moved in. A single lamp burned. There was very little furniture.

Maj supposed two automatons did not need much.

Maybell, however, gave off a clear air of distress.

"I told him he should not go out," she wailed. "When they broke the windows, I said he should stay safe inside. He said he needed to protect Officer Riley's property."

Maj could not argue with that, since Ben had done the same.

Ben said calmly, "Let us see whether he's operational."

After several minutes it became evident that Gamet was not. Though a good, steady fire still burned in his thorax, and steam leaked through several joints, his head had been smashed in at the forehead, and one arm was frozen in place.

"Oh. Oh!" Maybell wailed. "What has happened to him?"

"I don't know," Ben admitted. "I'm no tinker, but I'd

guess his—er—control center has been damaged."

"Why? Why would they do this to him? He never harmed anyone. We were just trying to have a—a life."

Through the broken windows came a shrill whistle. Maj could hear people yelling. What had happened here, so she realized, was also happening elsewhere.

She ran her hand down Maybell's arm, though she didn't know if the unit perceived it as an attempt at comfort. "I'm sure he can be repaired."

"Yes," Ben agreed. "I know of a very good repairman. We'll get him there tomorrow. It's not far."

Maybell moaned, a soft sound like a kettle just coming to the boil.

"Meanwhile, we'd better board up those windows if we can."

"Yeah, it's freezing."

"Maybell, do you know if there's any wood we can use? A hammer and nails?"

Maybell waved her hands helplessly.

"Perhaps the cellar," Maj suggested to Ben. "Is there a cellar?"

Leaving Maybell beside Gamet, still waving her hands, they went down a flight and into Riley's apartment to assess the damages there. More smashed windows, and a rock had crashed into a lamp, which also lay broken. Snow streamed in.

They found a doorway off the kitchen that led down to a cavernous cellar where they located not boards but cardboard Riley must have been saving for something, along with a hammer and some brass tacks.

"Better than nothing," Ben declared. "Help me carry it up."

Maj stood where she was, arrested. Here, below

ground, she could feel even more clearly the energies that ran beneath her feet. Or, they should be running. Flowing. Instead they bucked and tangled. A feeling of distress arose and swamped her like a miasma. She swayed where she stood.

The next thing she knew, Ben was calling her name. He sounded frantic, and his fingers dug into her shoulders.

"Maj? Maj!"

"I'm all right."

She lied, though, because she wasn't. She'd very nearly been pulled down into that dark confusion, straight into the disquiet.

"Look at me. Maj, look at me!"

He engaged her and at once she felt *him* rather than the fractured energy beneath her feet.

"Go upstairs. Get away from here. I'll bring the supplies."

"I can help."

"No. I don't want you down here."

She went, half tripping over her skirts in her haste, and he followed, dragging the cardboard. It took a while to cover over all the broken windows on both floors, and to sweep up the shattered glass. By the time they finished, neither Officer Riley nor his wife had returned home.

Maybell kept a vigil beside her frozen mate, whose fire still burned yet who remained unresponsive. *Just like Ben*, Maj startled herself by thinking. If Ben were to have another episode and died, that could be her.

Shocked by the realization and more disturbed than she could express, she and Ben at last went upstairs. Maj released Pup from the washroom.

"We were lucky," she said, surveying their own front windows.

"Too high for them to reach." Ben rubbed his forehead. "What a nightmare.

"Here, take off your coat. And your shirt."

"Maj. Now?"

"You took a tremendous thump to the shoulder."

"They were throwing pretty hard."

"I want to see what harm has been done."

"Just like an automaton?"

He wasn't steel and strong iron, though. He was flesh and bone. A bruise already bloomed on his left shoulder, dark purple with lighter colors flared around it.

All at once, Maj wanted to cry. "You were awfully brave. And awfully foolish."

He said nothing, just tipped up her chin so he could gaze into her eyes.

"It's so terrible." Her voice caught. "To hurt someone for no reason."

"I'm all right."

"You keep getting hurt. And I can't stop it."

"Hush, now. You're upsetting Pup."

True enough, the small animal pawed at Maj's skirt.

"Ben, I'm frightened." Not for herself but for him. For the damage spreading through the city this day. For what she felt beneath the ground.

Because with all the latent energies in such turmoil, how could she hope to heal the man she loved?

Chapter Twenty-Six

The story was splashed all over the front page of next morning's paper. Far-reaching damages in the city. Automaton-owned properties targeted. Numerous steam units unfortunate enough to have been out on the street battered and destroyed.

Ben picked up a copy of the paper on his way to work because Mayor Piffin had lifted the citywide shutdown. Ben hoped it wasn't because the mayor had been drinking too much Buffalo's Best Beer. He suspected, rather, it was because the ban had done no good—the marauders had been out in force anyway.

Ben hated, though, to part with Maj. He always hated to part with her, but right now something was very much amiss. He'd never seen her the way she'd been last night. Usually tough, edgy, and damned near fearless, she'd been shaken to the bone.

He'd seen that in her eyes and felt it in the way she touched him. It had started with her lips on his bruised shoulder and ended in the brass bed.

She'd needed him then in a fundamental way he'd sensed rather than consciously acknowledged. Needed him inside her, and wrapped around her.

Early in the evening, Riley had come home. Ben had dressed and run downstairs to talk with him.

The hybrid automaton, when he and his wife arrived home from a meeting she'd been attending at the

Automaton Liberation League, had accompanied Ben up to see the damaged Gamet and his partner. He expressed his gratitude to Ben for his help, and went on to describe the destruction across the city.

"Quite frankly, *sor*, I don't know what's to be done. People are calling for the mayor to step down, saying he's not capable of leading at such a troubled time."

"Yes, but who could lead the city through all this unrest?"

Ben saw nothing in the paper about recalling the mayor. Buffalo had been through several managers of late, the one before Piffin having been found corrupt.

When he reached Prospect Avenue, it looked quiet and peaceful, if half-clogged by snow. The bare trees shivered in a cold wind, and Mitch's house felt wondrously warm when he stepped in through the back door.

He met Mitch's wife, Tessa, coming out of Mitch's office when he went in. She once more carried her little mechanical dog, and smiled at him.

"Good morning, Mr. Ambrose." Her gaze marked the bandage on his brow, though she did not remark upon it. "Do you think things will get back to normal today?"

"Mrs. Carter. I'm not sure things will ever get back to normal again."

She nodded. "It's just awful. Who knows where all this trouble will end?"

She went off, and Ben stuck his head in Mitch's office. Mitch waved him in.

"What's happened to you?" Mitch asked, indicating Ben's bandage.

"Got caught up in that fight at the hockey game."

"Oh? I'm very sorry to hear that, since I gave you

the tickets. Nasty business. I hear the tournament's suspended for the time being. Mayor wants fewer people on the streets. We'd better get done what business we can, while we can."

He handed Ben a list. "Hit as many of these places as you can manage. Do you want to take one of the boys along?"

The boys denoted Mitch's regular crew, who might better be considered toughs than businessmen. A little muscle.

"You mean, as a bodyguard? I shouldn't need one, should I?" He met Mitch's shrewd gaze. "It sounds awful to say, but I should be all right, since I'm not an automaton."

Mitch shrugged. "It's possible to get in the crossfire—you're walking proof of that. Up to you."

"I'm not sure how it would look if I turn up at those inspections with—well, somebody intimidating at my back."

"All right. But at least take one of the cars. Safer and quicker getting around."

A good thought, but the steamcar Ben borrowed proved neither safer nor quicker. The streets were still a mess, all ruts and slush churned up by the hooves of the horses. Ben spent more time out helping the driver push than he did riding.

Around noon, he directed the driver to Virginia Street.

Dull sunshine, the color of copper, broke through the leaden gray skies as they parked, and it lit the houses to a rosy hue. A number of children were out front of the McMahon place, playing at pelting each other with snowballs, but Ben's house, next door, stood quiet.

"I'll be just a minute," he told the driver, Kurt. The man slid down in his seat and lit a cigar. "Take your time, Mr. Ambrose. I'd rather sit here than fight the streets."

Dora rolled into the entryway as Ben let himself into the house. The familiar scents of the place—old wood, furniture polish, and a faint whiff of coal smoke—assailed his nostrils, smelling of home.

"Oh, Mr. Benjamin!" Dora rasped at him through her aged voice box. "There have been such changes here. We have a new worker."

"Do you?"

"Yes. His name is Roland. He is currently in the cellar, shoveling the new delivery of coal.

"Working out, then, is he?" Ben pulled off his gloves. "Is my mother—"

"Benjamin! You've come home!"

His mother appeared from the parlor, her face troubled but with relief in her eyes. "Dora, bring some tea."

Dora trundled off, and Benjamin followed his mother into the other room.

"I haven't come home, Mother. I've just come to check that you're all right and pick up a few more things."

She turned to face him. "You're not staying?"

"I'm not, no. I'm working today, and afterward I'm returning to Congress Street."

"To that—woman?"

Ben said nothing.

His mother drew a breath. "I have to say—"

"No, you don't. Please."

"What's happened to your head? Did you have another episode?"

"No. Just a spot of trouble at the hockey game."

"I knew she'd get you in trouble. It's written all over her. Ben, I understand that young men can get caught up in—well," she blushed scarlet, "the moment. And you've never fallen victim before to—er—feminine wiles. But that girl, she's the last sort of female with whom you should get involved."

"Mother, I can't agree. Magenta is just exactly what I need."

"That is merely your impulses talking. If you've decided you want a wife, and I suppose you're of an age, there are plenty of nice, decent women with whom you might settle down."

"Magenta—"

"Who is she, Benjamin? Do you know anything about her background?"

"I know all I need to."

"I tell you, this is mere infatuation."

"I can't stay and argue it with you. I won't. Dora says the new steam unit arrived."

"Yes. You might have warned me. It was dropped off by the biggest, most terrifying unit I've ever seen."

"From Pike's Steam Repair, yes. Is he working out all right?"

"I suppose so. It shoveled the walks and Dora has it doing others of Winston's tasks."

"That's good."

Dora rattled in with the tea tray. "I'm afraid I can't stay," Ben told his mother. "Listen, are all Father's books still in his study?"

"I haven't touched a thing in there since he died."

"Good. I may have to borrow a few of them."

He went off to the study at the back of the house. To

his dismay, his mother followed.

"What do you want in here?"

The steam lamp came on with a hiss. The familiar room did indeed look untouched, right down to Father's spectacles still lying on the desk. Dora must have visited occasionally, for no dust lay anywhere. Row upon row of books lined the walls.

"Father had books about the city, didn't he? The history of it, I mean."

"Of course. As you know, he was deeply interested in everything from the architecture to the geological aspects of both Buffalo and Niagara Falls."

"Yes." Ben rapidly scanned the titles on the shelves. Some law books. Natural history. How would he find what he needed?

As he searched, Mother nattered on. "Your father was a personal acquaintance of Frederick Law Olmstead, who laid out the city. In fact, your father had considerable input."

"Did he, now?"

"Indeed. He always felt he had a deep and fundamental connection to Buffalo."

And I'm his son. Did that explain anything?

Ben stood with his eyes closed for an instant, feeling rather than seeing. The image of a section of bookcases appeared in his mind. One title slid out toward him. He opened his eyes and walked to it, to pull the volume from the shelf.

The Powers Beneath Us, it was called, by Rupert Edward Tollen. Just a small volume, well worn.

"I'm taking this one." He tucked it inside his coat.

"Take whatever you like. Just—"

He turned to face her. "Do you need anything,

Mother?"

"I need you to come home."

"I mean, food or supplies? If you do, send word to me. Don't send Dora out to the shops. Too many automatons are being attacked."

"Is there nothing I can say?"

"No." He went and embraced her.

She returned the hug, but looked at him unhappily. "Already she's changing you. You don't even look like yourself."

"Maybe that's good."

"How can it be good? You've got bandages on your head and you haven't even bothered to shave."

"I'm growing a beard."

"Well, frankly, I don't like it. You look like a—a vagrant. Just like her."

"Don't do this, Mother. Don't cause a rift between us."

"I'm not the one causing the rift, though of course you can't see that. I suppose I have to let you get it out of your system before you come home. Once you've come to your senses."

He hoped she wouldn't hold her breath.

Chapter Twenty-Seven

"What's that?" Maj leaned over Ben's shoulder where he sat in the overstuffed chair, and peered at the small volume in his hands. The print, as she could see, was very small. Yet he'd been absorbed in it ever since they finished supper.

Indeed, he looked up at her, his eyes looking foggy through his lenses. "You're right, they're called ley lines."

"What are?" Maj thought about it. "Oh, the streams of energy I can feel underground? The ones Dirk told me about?"

"Yes." He held out his hand to her and she squeezed into the chair with him, half in his lap.

"It says so right here. This was one of my father's books. He had all sorts of them. These ley lines, they exist all over the world. The ancients knew about them and used them, also, though much of that knowledge has been lost as of today."

"Used them? How?"

"To accomplish tremendous feats like raising Stonehenge. To perform magic."

"Magic."

"Yes. And a number of these lines do run here, just like your friend said, at the juncture of two great lakes. Beneath Buffalo."

"Well, I always knew they were there. I can feel

them."

"I suspect you're attuned. There have been people throughout the ages who were."

"Oh."

"Some of them, like Merlin, have become great mages."

"Mages. You mean—"

"Magicians." He laughed suddenly. "Even your name sounds a little like that, doesn't it? Maj."

"I was named by an old woman, a thief, because when I was a baby she could see a magenta-colored halo around me. Or so the story goes."

She eyed him. "You think we're connected with this, you and me?"

"It seems pretty evident, doesn't it? Look at this."

This proved to be a diagram on another page.

"A map of the area before anything was built here. The man who plotted out the ley lines that run here was a sensitive, like you."

"But it looks just like some of the streets." She touched the page. "You can almost see them. Here and here."

"I know. Apparently my father was acquainted with Frederick Law Olmstead, who laid out much of the city."

"Do you think your father had input in how it was laid out? Do you think he could feel these—these lines just as I can?"

"I don't know."

"Benjamin." A terrible feeling stole over Magenta. "How did your father die?"

"An—an attack of some kind. I thought it was his heart."

She drew away from him a little, staring at him in

dismay. "You don't think— Oh, Ben, no wonder your mother's so worried about your episodes."

Ben blinked. "I guess I never thought about it before. She told me he had an attack. I thought she meant a heart attack."

Dread rolled through Maj like sickness. If it were true, the same thing could happen to Benjamin at any time. The thing that had in fact already happened numerous times.

If it happened again, perhaps while they were apart, and she couldn't save him…

"How do we break free of this? This connection to these ley lines."

"I don't suppose we can. They've been there through millennia. Pure energy. As are we, some say."

"Topaz says that. She can see the energy inside all of us, see it with her inner, gypsy eye. She doesn't advertise that fact because of what people think of it, but it's true. She's always insisted I have a bit of the same ability."

"Yes."

"She can sense positive or negative energy in a person. What's more, that energy survives after death. The body is just—well, like an automaton. In fact she says she can sense the same energy from automatons. It's a lot fainter, but it's there."

"So we're all the same beneath the skin, or beyond the metal. Why are we fighting each other?"

"Sheer pigheadedness, I'd say. We all want to insist we're right."

Pup jumped up on Ben's knee and nuzzled into Maj's lap.

"Some people," she mused then, "you can just feel

the positive energy coming off them. Like Jamie Kilter. And so many others in the city. But there's darkness, too, like Jamie Kilter when he loses his temper."

"Like those people who smashed the windows."

"And battered the automatons, yes."

They both fell silent, thinking.

"So," Maj said after a moment, "if all this is true," she tapped the book, "how do we fix it?"

****

That question continued to haunt Maj while she tried to sleep, and even invaded her dreams. She felt as if she battled unseen forces, unstoppable as a tremendous wave off the lake.

It was the wind that woke her sometime later. She opened her eyes and stared into the dark air of the bedroom. Benjamin lay beside her, breathing low and steady, and Pup slept across her feet.

The wind howled. It sounded like a steam train huffing past outside the windows, screaming as it went. Every time a gust seized the house it rocked, making the bed upon which they lay quiver like jelly.

Alarm punched through her and set all her senses to pricking. No ordinary wind this, but an angry and violent menace.

"Ben?"

Pup raised his head from her feet and whined. She reached down and stroked him reassuringly.

"All right, boy."

She slid from the warm bed and, with Pup following, padded out to the parlor. Usually the house felt at least reasonably warm. Now though, a penetrating cold struck through the very walls like the touch of death.

She knelt on one of the window seats and rubbed at

the glass, which had iced over on the inside. Was something wrong with the steam plant down in the cellar? They had their own coal fire, but it had died back after they went to bed.

She could see very little through the glass besides darkness. A sound behind her made her turn her head.

"Magenta? What is it?"

"I think the blizzard has arrived."

He came up behind her, his warmth a shield. He put one knee on the window seat and tried to look out. A gust struck the side of the house, which swayed like a tree.

"Jesus," he whispered.

"A little scary up here, isn't it?"

He wrapped his arms around her in comfort. "I'm sure it will look better in daylight."

****

Only, daylight was slow in coming. Though the ugly clock on the mantel counted out the hours, it never truly grew bright outside.

And though it scarcely seemed possible, the wind just worsened.

From a series of vicious gusts, it morphed into a steadily screaming banshee that hurled out of the southwest. As soon as Maj scraped the ice off the insides of the windows in an attempt to peer out, more formed and made a thick coating, preventing either of them from seeing much. Ben lit the coal fire in the grate, and Maj made tea. At around six, they got dressed in their outer garments to take Pup outside.

On their way out they encountered Michael Riley, clad for outdoors. At first Ben thought he meant to go out and shovel.

"You won't make much progress out there," Ben

told him above the harsh wail of the wind. Through the glass in the front door, which had been replaced, he could see little more than a stream of snow—flying sideways.

Riley shook his head. "I'm on duty."

"Surely not."

"People will be stranded. Needing help."

Ben took another look outside. "Even you won't be able to withstand that for long."

"So long as the fire in my thorax keeps burning, I should be all right. Anyway, it's not about me, is it, *sor*? I would appreciate it if you'd hold the fort here while I'm gone. Look after those on the second floor and Felicity, who is staying home today. I don't know when I'll be back."

As if on cue, Felicity put her head out their door. As much as a hybrid could, she looked worried.

"Of course we will," Ben assured Riley.

Riley went on, "I've loaded the steam plant in the cellar with coal and it should hold for a while. It's doing its job, but the warmth is just being blown out of the house."

Wouldn't the same thing happen to Riley, when he went out in this? Benjamin wondered. Under it all, Riley was in truth a mobile steam plant. If his fire did blow out and he went down in the snow, what would happen to his organic components, his eyes and skin covering?

Perhaps driven by a similar concern, Felicity tiptoed out. "Husband, I wish you would not go out. Surely Captain Fagan will not expect it."

Not without tenderness, Riley told her, "I expect it of myself, my love. If I am not a policeman, what am I?"

"My husband."

"That too. Have faith in the strength of my metal. In

the power of the steam. I will return."

They all three watched him go out the front door, a big, strapping figure who nonetheless swayed when the wind took him.

Ben very nearly called him back. No one, nothing could be expected to survive out in that white wasteland.

But if Riley would not stay for Felicity, he would not stay for Ben.

Ben blinked, and Riley disappeared into the blur of streaming snow as if he'd never been.

Felicity moved to return to her flat, and Maj placed a hand on her arm. "Why don't you come upstairs with us for a while? We're just going to take Pup out and will be right back. It may help pass the time if—"

"Thank you, no. It is kind, but—" Very quietly, Felicity returned to her flat and closed the door softly.

"What do you think she does in there, Ben? All alone."

Ben shrugged. "I hate to think. Listen, you stay here and keep watch. I'll take Pup out."

"Absolutely not. We all go."

He nodded, picked Pup up, and they pushed their way outside.

Even though Ben was prepared for an onslaught, or thought he was, he promptly lost all breath. The wind, brutal and merciless, snatched it from him and flew away with it. Tiny icy particles drove into his face. His eyes immediately began to stream and sting.

He looked around for a place to set Pup. There, in the lee of some whitened bushes, was a patch where the snow had been blown away. Stumbling to it, with Maj clinging on behind him, he carefully placed the shivering, bewildered animal down.

Maj tried to say something. The words, torn from her mouth, winged away.

Whether Pup relieved himself or not, Ben couldn't tell. He snatched the animal back up and together, now against the wind, they fought their way back to the door and manhandled their way inside where they stood gasping and staring at one another.

The city had already been in uproar. What might this dire event do to it?

Chapter Twenty-Eight

Time passed, and yet it didn't. Maj felt as if she'd fallen into an internal doldrum, a place in the backwaters apart from the normal current of time. Though the sun presumably rose, you wouldn't know it, for it existed to little effect somewhere beyond the storm.

Worse, she could feel the disruption the storm created. In herself, in Benjamin, on the city and the energies that flowed beneath it. Snarled and diverted, just like time, they no longer flowed.

She could not settle. She worried about Benjamin and the physical effects of this profound mayhem upon him. What if his spiritual condition deteriorated to the point that he died? Here with her, alone. Would she know what to do? Could she bring him back?

She wished she'd focused more on understanding and developing her innate abilities. Ever since they'd met, Topaz had encouraged her to do just that, and had implied it was key to her survival.

We may not be able to deny what's inside us, Magenta. But we can come to terms with it and find some peace.

Maj, though, had opted for denial. Right up till the moment she met Ben. Now she'd give all she was to help him. But she wasn't sure how.

It grew steadily colder in the house. Ben went down to the cellar and fetched more coal for their fire, and when he didn't come back right away, Maj followed him. She found him standing, speaking with Maybell, on the floor beneath them. Due to the weather, Michael Riley had not been able to take Gamet in for repair, so Maybell was stranded alone with the inoperative unit.

"It must be awful, having him standing there damaged," he remarked to Maj on their way back upstairs. "Even worse than for Felicity being left alone. I feel responsible for them."

Maj nodded, but she felt sick inside. All her own emotions focused on Ben, and she had to find a way to handle them. It wasn't fair for her to cling to and potentially smother him.

Yet the only ease she found came when they cuddled in the overstuffed chair together, his arms around her and Pup at their feet.

"The bad thing is," Ben remarked at one point, "we're so isolated. We don't know what's going on." He jerked his head at the window. "Out there."

When Maj said nothing, he went on. "No way to get a message to anyone. No hope of seeing a newspaper."

"I imagine everyone is just battened down. It's fortunate, I guess, the blizzard hit at night. Most people will have been at home."

"Yes. But it's as Riley said, there will be emergencies. People in need of help. Of a physician's care. And if anyone did get caught outside—"

"They won't last long," Maj murmured.

When the clock on the mantel read noon, Ben told her, "Why don't you check on Felicity and Maybell? I'll take Pup outside."

Yet when he attempted to carry the small animal out front, a four-foot high drift blocked his path.

Felicity, who had answered her door to Maj, called, "Come through here. You can take the animal out back. It may be more sheltered."

It was, but only a little. Maj watched through the window in the door while Ben, using a shovel he'd found in Felicity's back hall, cleared a three-foot space for Pup to use.

She held her breath while he remained outside, seeing in her mind's eye an image of him falling to the ground, caught by one of his episodes.

He came back in with his eyes streaming from the wind and his face chapped red. He had to sit on a chair in Felicity's kitchen to catch his breath.

"I think the wind's got worse," he said once he could speak. "I know that's hard to believe."

"I hope Michael is safe at the police station," Felicity fretted, clasping her hands together. "Though I do not suppose he will be. He will be out in that weather—trying to help others."

Maj asked her with sympathy, "Are you sure you don't want to come up and visit with us for a while?"

"I would not be good company."

"That doesn't matter."

But Felicity refused to be persuaded. "Please feel free to take your animal out through my apartment whenever you need to."

"We will." It would give Maj a good chance to check on the hybrid automaton.

Upstairs she turned on Ben and looked him in the eye. "Are you all right?"

"Of course." He shrugged out of his coat but quickly dodged her searching stare. "Why wouldn't I be?"

Fiercely she told him, "I can feel you, you know.

193

Feel what's going on with your energies. If it's true you're connected to the city—well the city's in a bad way right now, isn't it?"

He said nothing but his lips compressed into a thin line.

Her heart began to pound. "Don't you lie to me, Benjamin Ambrose. How do you really feel?"

To her alarm, he laid one palm against his chest. "Honestly? A bit low, maybe. The wind stole my breath, that's all, and my chest feels raw where the cold air went in."

"You need a shot of whiskey. We don't have any, darn it."

"I'll be fine."

She took a step closer to him. "If your energies are low, I'll give you mine."

That said, she kissed him. As an attempt to pour herself into him, it proved singularly effective. She felt him strengthen and take light.

"Come on." She towed him to the other room, and to the bed.

****

Ben hadn't wanted to admit it, especially to Maj who as he could clearly tell was worried about him. But by the time he'd returned inside with Pup and they climbed the stairs back to their apartment, he felt a tingling starting in his feet. He told himself it was due to having been out in the cold. His feet were merely numb.

Only what he'd begun to experience hadn't been simple numbness so much as the onslaught of something far worse.

He knew that sensation and how it felt to die.

He couldn't admit that to Magenta, though. He could

194

already see the fear in her eyes. Fear for him. That wasn't what he wanted to bring to her.

In the bedroom, though, she stripped him down to his smalls, pulled him beneath the covers and set about— well, he supposed warming him was the best description. Forming a connection that lifted and secured him. She lavished kisses on his face, his neck, shoulders, and chest, moving ever downward. Outside, the wind shrieked so loudly he could hear nothing else, not even Maj's breaths as she caressed him. Up at the top of the house as they were, caught in the teeth of the storm, it felt like a battle between Magenta and chaos.

No ordinary lovemaking, this. She claimed him over again. She fought for him, for his very soul.

He once more lost track of time. The steam lamp sputtered out and the light in the room faded to gray. Maj drew him to her using her mouth and hands. She wooed him and stirred him, made him forget everything except desire. Then she drew him inside her and held him there.

Held him while he came into line.

When he hummed inside, louder almost than the wind, he opened his eyes and looked at her.

Her eyes remained closed, dark lashes spread against her warm, golden skin, her face wreathed with bliss. He marveled at her beauty, an unusual sort of splendor that perhaps the world could not appreciate. And at how, rather than two separate beings, they had now become one.

Then she opened her eyes, and he gasped at what he saw there.

"Don't move." She curled her fingers into him, hanging on. For dear life.

He had no intention of moving. Here lay everything.

The roots of existence. Life itself.

She said fiercely, "So long as you stay inside me, we are safe. And I can't lose you, understand?"

"I understand. Don't worry, you won't lose me." He shouldn't tell her that. It could happen. He could die at any time.

If she let him. But she wouldn't.

Accepting that truth, everything within him eased. He relaxed against her small, powerful body.

"That's better. Everything's back in place."

"Yes."

A smile ignited in her black eyes. "All I have to do, to keep you safe, is keep making love to you."

"I'm on board with that."

"Quite possibly, that's all we need to do in order to keep the whole city safe."

"I'm willing to make whatever sacrifice."

She laughed.

"The storm will have to let up eventually, won't it?"

"Shows no signs yet."

"No, but it will have to blow out. Then—what will we find outside?"

"Drifts of snow higher than my head. And a whole lot of empty Buffalo's Best Beer bottles."

"That's all right, then."

He closed his eyes and drifted back into the sea of bliss. He could feel Maj, all of her, from the place he rested outward. Inward too, to her spirit. A fierce thing that would fight like a tiger for him.

Let it flow.

For several long minutes, he did that, until he felt her lips on one side of his mouth, then the other.

"Again," she whispered, and he grew hard inside

her.

"Again? It's like magic."

"It is magic. A very potent kind of magic. And it's our duty to indulge it here amid the storm. To save the city."

"Snow City," he mused and fell into her once more.

Chapter Twenty-Nine

The blizzard raged on. Screaming out of the southwest, it howled down the immense length of Lake Erie's dark, frozen waters and scooped up in its arms the snow piled mile upon mile by consecutive snowstorms all the way back to November.

Without mercy it dumped the snow upon the city, piling it high against the walls of factories, grain elevators, and warehouses. It cast the snow full force at churches and in the faces of houses, making them tremble to their foundations. It clogged narrow back streets. It froze whatever and whomever it encountered, to the steel or to the bone.

No one caught out in it would deny it had a personality, and possibly a malevolence. Some fell before it. Some rested beneath it. All those who heard it raging from within four walls huddled, wondering if it would ever end.

In the bed at the top of the house on Congress Street, Maj stirred and wondered what had happened to her. Because if she knew one thing amid the storm and the general madness, it was that she had changed. Everything had changed.

Not that she'd ceased to be the child who had spent her extreme youth with a snotty nose, filthy, and dressed in rags. Or who'd spent her childhood and adolescence perfecting the art of thievery. She hadn't. That girl, that

Magenta, still dwelt inside her and lent her muscle to the battle they now fought.

It was just that she'd become so much more. A woman. A woman with her fingers on the strands of an energy that drove the world. One who could employ magic, even if only at the most primitive level. She was the energy. And it was her. She could no longer deny that.

She could no longer deny a number of things. That, try as she might, she could not cut herself off from the world. That, try as she always had, she could not protect herself from the possibility of loss.

When one loved, one embraced the probability of pain. And she—oh, she loved.

Benjamin stirred in the bed and opened his deep chocolate eyes. They held an expression of lazy possessiveness she liked to see. He had the right. He owned her, body and soul.

"Have you just been lying there all quiet?" she asked. "I thought you were sleeping."

"I was watching you sleep. I like it when you're at rest, Maj. It doesn't happen too often."

"Only with you. Only ever with you."

"I guess even a ball of energy has to calm down eventually."

She'd poured so much of herself into him, to keep him topped up, so to speak, she could hardly be anything but calm.

With one arm bent behind his head, Ben wove the fingers of his other hand through her hair. His touch felt like heaven.

"I suppose," he said, still lazily, "we'll have to get dressed and take Pup out."

"I'll go," she said quickly. "Not you."

"Magenta." His fingers, still in her hair, stopped stroking. "You can't protect me forever."

"I can. I will."

"No."

"Ben, I'm afraid something's going to happen. With the storm and the forces below the city all snarled up the way they are… If something happened to you, what would I do? I love you."

She pressed her mouth to his and closed her eyes so she couldn't read what lay in his. A terrible thing, a terribly potent thing, confessing love. Something she'd never, ever done.

"Magenta, darling." He ended the kiss so he could study her. "I love you too, though in truth there are no words for what I feel for you. None."

Her heart leaped at him gifting the declaration back to her, before doubt rushed in. "Maybe you don't want l-love from someone like me, nothing more than a street brat when it comes down to it."

"I want you. I want your love. Nothing else."

"Because you're all respectable and I'm—I'm not."

"I was respectable. Now I'm just yours. Whatever you make of me."

"But—"

"Magenta, you saying you love me makes me humble. It makes me grateful."

"I've never loved anyone before."

"That's why it makes me humble."

"I'll never love anyone else this way, not ever again."

"You don't know that."

"I do."

"We didn't know we'd find this, did we?"

"No. But I'm so afraid. I can't lose you."

"Hush."

"Ben, I—"

Hush.

He kissed her again, perhaps to halt her words. He slid his lips down from her lips over her chin, down here neck, and latched onto her breast. Euphoria came and, yes, halted all words. Halted even the need for them.

"I must confess I'm hungry," he murmured as he moved from one breast to the other. "Hungry for you. All right?"

"Yes. Anything."

And she thought, as he slid his mouth down her body and gently parted her thighs, if the storm went on forever, that just might be all right.

****

Michael Riley never came home. At least they never heard him enter the house. Late in the afternoon when Ben accompanied Maj to take Pup outside and they sought admittance through the ground floor apartment, they found Felicity still alone, and worried.

"Michael should have finished his shift long since," she fretted when they brought Pup back in. "He should be home."

"I'm sure he's just been delayed," Ben sought to reassure her.

"Perhaps. There will be emergencies on every hand, and Michael always puts helping others ahead of all else. But so much could have happened to him."

Maj touched Felicity's arm comfortingly. "Try not to think about that."

"I do not seem able to help it. In the past when he was delayed, he has sent me a message. That is not possible now."

"Would you like us to stay with you a while?"

"Perhaps."

"Maj, you sit with Mrs. Riley and I'll go down and check the steam plant, make sure it's operating properly." Try to find out why the house felt so cold.

In the cellar, Ben discovered the steam plant ran at top capacity, pumping out heat at a furious rate. The heat it produced, however, dissipated before reaching the top floor. He shoveled in more coal and went up to discover Michael Riley just coming in.

The hybrid automaton showed the effects of his ordeal in the storm. When he unwound the scarf from around his neck and removed the coat he wore over his blue uniform, he revealed white patches on the skin of his face and hands.

Felicity flew to him. They made a handsome couple, Ben had to admit—Riley with his fair hair and Felicity with her graceful bearing and slightly disheveled auburn mane. When they stood so, clasped in one another's arms, it was difficult to tell they weren't human.

Michael's fondness for his wife and her relief at having him home screamed aloud. If the automaton-haters of the city could see them like this, would it make a difference? Ben wondered.

"I cannot stay for long," Riley said. "Captain Fagan is sending us home in turns to get warmed through and see to our families. I have another shift in three hours."

"What's it like out there?" Maj asked.

Riley shook his head. "Vicious. I doubt the city has ever seen the like. Most of the side streets are completely blocked. The main thoroughfares are barely negotiable, mostly because of stranded vehicles that are now covered in snow. I have spent the day checking those vehicles for trapped passengers, of which there were many." His blue eyes, of course, did not change expression even when he said, "Five dead so far."

Ben felt the horror go through Maj at that. She seized his hand, her fingers tense.

Riley went on, "We got the survivors to shelter when we could. Although my fire kept burning well, I could feel my exterior temperature dropping. However, it was difficult to stop the search when each new mound of snow might conceal a buried vehicle and people needing rescue."

He gazed at Felicity. "I hope I have not done permanent damage to my outer skin."

"Let me see." She held up his hands and examined the whitened patches, her head cocked to one side as if she consulted her artificial intelligence. "I will bathe these areas with solution. She glanced at Maj and Ben. "We have a nutrient wash we must use on our organic layers. Beneath the skin we are steel and fire. But the outer layers are more fragile than you would think. Michael, if some of this skin dies, I am sure our physicians can graft more on."

"Perhaps." Riley shrugged. "Perhaps not."

"We will leave you to it." Ben tugged on Maj's hand. "Riley, I just checked the boiler in the cellar. You needn't bother with that. Once the snow stops, I'll get out after that drift outside the front door."

"Yes. No use attempting it now. The wind has made drifts of ten feet and more in places. And I would not have you risk yourself, *sor*."

"As you are doing?" Ben quirked a brow.

"It is my job, *sor*. And my calling. The situation

might have been much worse. The folks we are rescuing are those on their way home from night shifts, or from taverns and such places. Only think what this would have been like had it hit at midday. As it is, most people were already at home."

Ben nodded.

"They're saying a storm of this magnitude may not strike again for a hundred years."

"I hope not," Ben muttered as Maj pulled him back upstairs. "Once every hundred years is more than enough."

Chapter Thirty

The wind began to ease at nightfall, though in this instance *nightfall* was a relative thing, since it had never truly grown light all day long. At first Maj thought she merely imagined the waning intensity, because gusts still struck the side of the house. Those gusts were perhaps slightly less violent than they had been.

But her ears were not deceived. Gradually, the freight-train-level howling of the wind, which had for twenty-four hours been near constant, died to a wail.

She went to the window and chipped the ice off with her fingernail in an attempt to peer out.

"It's too dark to see much. Do you think it's letting up?"

Ben came and knelt on the window seat beside her. "Maybe."

"It's hard to imagine a whole city lying out there buried in white, isn't it? But I think I can feel it. The city, I mean. Can you? Blocks and blocks of houses and the streets like Riley said, all clogged up." She closed her eyes for an instant. "And under it all, it's gone quiet." Her eyes flew open again and she looked at Ben in alarm. "Do you feel quite well?"

His gaze fled hers. He got up and moved away from the window.

"Benjamin?" Maj's fear made her breathless. In all the years of her life, ever since she'd begun sensing the energies beneath her feet, she'd never felt them so still. And if he were in truth connected to those energies—

"I'm fine."

"Are you sure?"

He turned back and caught her shoulders between his hands. "Magenta, if we're to be together—are we to be together?"

"Yes," she said swiftly.

"—you can't spend your life, our lives, endlessly worrying about me. The city has temporarily ground to a halt, that's what you're feeling."

She licked her lips and stared into his eyes, trying to gauge it, to measure him. "Admit it. You're feeling low again."

He wanted to deny it. She saw the impulse flare in his eyes. "A bit depleted perhaps."

"But—not the way you do when you are about to—to die?" she whispered that last word, half afraid to speak it aloud.

He shook his head.

She fought down the panic. It would do neither of them any good. He was right, they couldn't live their lives hanging by a thread.

"Let's get some rest." He took her by the hand. "Now that the wind is dying down, maybe we'll sleep better."

She nodded. A part of her, though, would remain on guard all night long.

****

Ben awoke some time later to silence. In fact he suspected it was the cessation of sound that had roused him. For a day and a night the angry howling of the wind had filled his ears, and the trembling of the house had transmitted itself to him.

Now there was a deep hush, one that seemed to extend across the city and the land itself. He lay and listened to it. He couldn't even hear the thump of the steam plant in the cellar, and the air felt sharply cold.

Miraculously, though, Maj lay beside him fast asleep. She'd stirred several times during the night and laid her palm against his chest as if feeling for the beat of his heart.

Ben knew very well what she feared. She feared if the city went quiet like this, so would he.

Swiftly he tried to determine how he felt. He'd experienced dying more than a dozen times and had what might be called an instinct for it. Did he feel that way now, as if death laid hold of him?

Hard to say, because he felt so different from the way he had before he met Magenta. She'd changed him. Enlivened and completed him. Her fierce spirit reached out and embraced his.

Would that be enough?

At Maj's feet, Pup stirred and crawled up onto Ben's chest. Ben lay and stroked the little dog, wondering not for the first time what would become of Maj if something happened to him.

That was the trouble, wasn't it, with loving someone? It introduced the specter of loss, and that specter haunted Maj with her every breath.

He had to do his best to live, for her. But yes, he could feel forces pulling him down. Just like the city, would his body grind to a halt?

Difficult to imagine everything going on without him. An individual, be he made of flesh and bone or metal, or a combination of the two, saw everything through his own perspective, through the windows of his eyes, so to speak. When an automaton shut down, the world ended for it. It was the same for a man. Though intellectually Ben knew the world would continue if he died, he couldn't quite wrap his mind around it.

The world only existed, did it not, through his personal perception?

He lay and tried to accept it—that the world and everything in it could exist without him. The air in the room grew light and not a sound broke the silence beyond their rooms. The steam plant never kicked on. He should get dressed and go down to the cellar and find out why.

Yet he continued to lie there stroking Pup, Maj a bundle of warmth at his side, and listened to the hush.

Eventually he heard a door close downstairs. Someone else stirred in the house. A few streets away, a dog barked. Pup picked up his head.

Deep in the bowels of the house, the steam plant rumbled to life. Beside Ben, Maj stirred. He felt it the instant she woke, her awareness flaring like sparks inside him.

Her hand groped across his chest and pressed tight. "Ben?"

"I'm here, love."

"It's so quiet."

"Storm's over. Of course the cleanup's going to be a hell of a thing."

She sat up. "It will, won't it? I doubt the city will ever be the same."

****

"Nothing's moving," said Michael Riley when Maj and Ben met him on their way to take Pup outside. "I've never seen the like."

Riley had obviously just come home and still wore his coat, hat, and boots. He held a shovel in one hand.

Maj thought about it. No trolleys, no steamcabs or drays. No horse-drawn carriages, for that matter. No factories belching coal smoke into the sky. No newspapers or other forms of communication.

She asked Riley, "How much snow is there, all told?"

"Miss, it is impossible to calculate. The back yard is sheltered. You may take your dog there. Behind it, near the property line, is a drift higher than my head. And another out front. Egress from the front is blocked for now, as are all the walkways. And the street."

How would they ever clear it all away? Maj didn't know, but she needed the city to wake up and return to its normal, breathing, living self so Ben could return to his normal, vital self also.

She could feel that something inside him wasn't right. He didn't want to admit to it, but it terrified her.

Was she going to lose him? When she'd only just found him. After a lifetime of wanting, was she destined to have him for only this handful of days?

No. *No*.

Riley gestured outside. "I intend to work my way around to the front with my shovel, and attack the drift there."

Ben protested, "You can't do that all single-handed. Let me help."

"No." Maj said it aloud this time.

Michael Riley cocked his head at her. Could he detect her fear? "*Sor*, that won't be necessary."

"You have another shovel, don't you? I thought I

saw one in the back hallway."

"Yes, *sor*. But the temperature outside is still dangerously low."

"Look," Ben insisted, "if we're going to get through this, everyone in the city will have to work together."

"You're right, *sor*," Riley agreed. "But will they? That is the question."

Ben gave a rueful smile. "You and I can. It's a start."

"True, *sor*. And given that, I would be very glad of your assistance."

He went out with his shovel. Maj, Ben, and Pup followed, and while Pup took care of his business Maj seized hold of the man she loved by both arms.

"Have you lost your mind, Benjamin? You're talking about shoveling out drifts that are ten feet high. You're already depleted, as you call it. And it's not unknown for perfectly healthy men to suffer a heart attack while—"

He interrupted her, his brown eyes stony behind the foggy spectacles. "I am a perfectly healthy man."

"Physically, yes. But—"

"Spiritually, I may be low at the moment. The whole city's gone quiet. But I have to be able to live my life, or what's the point?"

Tears stung Maj's eyes. "I thought *I* was the point. *We're* the point."

"Yes. But there can be no *we* without me. You can't keep me dampered down like a—a steam plant. I'll be no good to either of us."

It was foolish. Maj knew that. She wanted to protect him. She wanted to weep and wail and stamp her foot in the snow.

She could no more do that than she could go out

front and shut Michael Riley down. A man, just like an automaton, had a right to his choices.

But tears still blurred her vision and froze on her eyelashes as she picked Pup up in her arms and went inside.

Chapter Thirty-One

For miles, all that could be heard was the scraping of shovels on ice-laden snow. A good thing, Ben decided as he worked plying his own shovel, yet uncanny also. He paused from time to time to catch his breath and to listen.

Michael Riley, who'd informed him he was off duty today, worked ahead of him, chopping away at the monstrous snowdrift that blocked the front of his house, while Ben labored at the walkways. He could glimpse Riley from time to time, until they shoveled snow onto the patch of lawn so high it blocked the line of sight.

Not easy work, hoisting every shovel full of snow shoulder high, and Ben felt it. He wondered from time to time if Maj wasn't right and he should go into the house for a rest.

But he needed to be a part of this.

The sun came out, dazzling on the snow so he had to squint his eyes nearly shut. He could hear neighbors working at the houses on either side but could not see them either.

Not a vehicle or horse or pedestrian went down Congress Street. Well, as he could see when he worked his way that far, the street was no longer a street so much as a trench filled side to side with solid snow. Granted, since the wind had been the true culprit during the blizzard, that snow was deeper in some spots than others.

It would all have to be cleared.

How would such a task be accomplished? It boggled the mind. But till the streets were all cleared, the city could not rumble back to life. And until the city rumbled back to life, the energy that lay so dormant, frozen, could not resume its flow.

The one relied on the other in some deep, mysterious way he did not truly understand.

Magenta came picking her way down the path he had shoveled, Pup at her heels. When she reached him she gazed around as if regarding a new world.

"This is strange!"

"It is, isn't it?" Ben paused and leaned on his shovel.

She eyed him up and down. "Let me help out here."

"I don't think Riley has any more shovels."

"Then let me have a turn with yours. You take Pup back inside and get warm."

"You'll need to lift the snow near as high as your head."

"I don't care." To his surprise and dismay, tears once more flooded her eyes. "It's too quiet. You're too quiet. You think I can't feel what's going on inside you?"

"Magenta." He laid his gloved hand on her shoulder and searched for words. "If I truly am part of this city, I have to be part of it. Do you think I want to go on living if it means I close myself in a room, away from everything?"

"What about me? What about what I want? Don't I count for anything?" she wailed.

"Of course you do—"

"Do you think I could go on living without you?"

Ben wondered a bit madly whether the neighbors on either side could hear them. The nearest shovels had stopped scraping. Michael Riley, at least, listened.

He cupped Maj's cheek. "I think you are strong. One of the strongest people I've ever known. You'd go on."

"You're wrong! I'd crumple into pieces, curl into a little ball without you. I'd be on my knees, weeping."

"Darling." He closed his eyes an instant, searching for the ties that bound them to one another. *There*. But she was right, the energy flowed very low, and slow.

The wall of snow beside them bellied and shattered. Riley had worked his way from the front drift and broken through. As far as a hybrid automaton could, he looked concerned.

"Mr. Ambrose, I would not be after wanting you to damage yourself. Maybe your lady is right and ye should go inside. Felicity or Maybell can come out for a while."

"I'm fine," Ben insisted.

"Mr. Ambrose, please be reasonable." Riley waved his arm. "There's a whole city to be cleared, for you can be certain this much snow will not go away by itself, not in January, and it would take the sun weeks even at its warmest. Sure, you'll have plenty of opportunities to do your bit."

Frustration seized Ben in a hard grip. He did not like being treated as an invalid, especially by his friends.

"Please, Ben." Maj looked a bit wildly at Riley. "I'll run and ask Felicity to come out, shall I?"

"Aye, and take the wee dog if he's finished his business. His paws will freeze."

She darted off. Ben and Riley stood looking at each other.

"'Tis not as if I don't appreciate your help," Riley said then. "If the city's to be put to rights, 'twill take all of us working together, as ye said earlier. Flesh and metal, and those of us who harbor both. But I understand too what it means to need. That young lady needs you, *sor*. 'Twould be a kindness to go inside with her for a while."

Kindness. Remarkable for an automaton to speak of it, especially after all the antagonism they had endured.

Of what did a *being* consist? Topaz had told Magenta she could sense spiritual energy not just from humans but from automatons, also. Maybe it was time to stop thinking of them as other, and recognize the sameness.

I'll go in for a while," Ben told Riley, "but I'll be back out for another turn."

"That's your choice, *sor*. We all have our own choices to make."

Felicity, well-bundled, came out and took the shovel from Ben. "Thank you, neighbor. I'm well-stocked with coal and ready to do my part with my husband."

Michael Riley emitted a curious sound that must be his version of laughter. "Are we not fortunate to have so many willing hands?"

He went back to his snowdrift and Felicity set to on the end of the walkway. Maj wriggled her fingers into Ben's.

"Come on."

They would have to talk about this, they truly would. He could not have the woman he loved treating him like an invalid. But for her sake, he followed her inside.

****

Ben was upset with her, Maj could tell. The truth was, she could feel everything about him—when he took each breath, when his mood turned, and when his thoughts moved. That was precisely what worried her so much.

She did not want him angry with her, if anger correctly described his current state of mind. Annoyed might be closer to accurate. Aggravated. Frustrated.

He didn't like being told what to do. Who did? Not her, certainly. In fact it had always been one of her failings, that she tended to do the opposite of what she was told.

Ben wasn't like that, though. He was sensible and even-tempered. Her opposite.

Except—now his energies burned low and he might not be entirely himself.

Dared she attempt to pour herself into him once again? She wondered as she bustled around the flat, pretending she couldn't see that he sat and brooded. He did not seem in the mood, at the moment, for making love.

Upset with her, yes. He felt trapped and confined. She never wanted him to feel imprisoned by her love.

So even though she ordinarily possessed a glib tongue, she didn't know what to say now. Instead she made the tea and straightened the cloth on the table.

Then she went and perched on the arm of the chair where he sat.

"Do not be angry with me." Maj stared into the warm, chocolate-brown eyes, so full of emotions they nearly overflowed. She needed him to feel their connection.

"I'm not angry. It's just—Maj, it can't be like this between us."

"This?"

"You seeking to protect me. My parents strove to do that all my life. And after my father died, Mother took it over with a vengeance. I've had my fill of that. I'm not a child. I'm a man, and I need an equal footing with you."

Maj drew a breath. "I understand that. I respect that. But, Ben, it's hard. I'm so afraid of losing you. Think on it. You came to me in order to find a way to keep from dying. A cure of sorts. All I've done is fall in love with you. How will I ever handle the guilt if—"

"No guilt can be attributed to you, Magenta."

"It's easy to say that."

He took her hand in his. "Despite the reason I came to you in the first place, it's not your responsibility to keep me alive."

"It is! More than that, it's my desire. Keeping you alive keeps me alive in turn. Don't you see that?"

Tears tumbled unheeded down her cheeks. And that upset her even more. She rarely allowed herself to show this kind of vulnerability.

He thumbed her tears away, leaned in, and kissed her.

"I'm not angry with you," he repeated.

She tried to believe it.

Chapter Thirty-Two

Ben did another stint with the shovel that afternoon. Magenta insisted on taking her turn after that, followed by Maybell and Felicity once more. Michael Riley just kept on shoveling, moving the white drifts away from the walls of his house like—well, like the machine Ben supposed he was.

It became so there was nowhere to put the snow. The small, square yard in front of the house was piled high, as was the strip of lawn between the sidewalk and the street. The shoveled sidewalks turned into tunnels open to the sky with no view to one side or the other.

Riley had cleared a path between his house and the next, and Ben had himself extended it to what should be the street. It ended, however, in a wall of snow.

Maj had just come outside with Pup when Ben paused at the end of that path, and they encountered an incredible sight.

In truth, Ben heard it first, something beyond the seemingly endless scrape of shovels. This, too, was a variety of scraping but far louder and more continuous.

Maj paused with Pup at her heels and looked at Ben. Michael Riley walked back from his post near the front door, which he'd managed to clear, at length. And Pup, who'd just left a yellow decoration in the newly shoveled snow, gave a sharp bark.

Down Congress Street came... At first glance Ben

didn't know what it was. It possessed a great number of legs all stepping in time, and it shed show right and left the way the prow of a ship sheds water.

A wall. A moving wall of shovels. A wall of shovels plied by automatons.

They were four or five deep and they filled the street from side to side. At the front came a row of hybrids, most of them dressed in the blue uniforms of Buffalo Police officers.

Ben recognized members of the Irish Squad whom he had encountered before. Terry Greely, along with other familiar faces, and front and center, the prow of the plow, so to speak, Officer Pat Kelly.

They stopped in front of Riley's house. Riley, Maj, Ben, and Pup went out to meet them.

There, in the bright sunlight that had followed the storm, the hybrids looked hale and hearty, and the rows of metal automatons who followed glittered and shone with spots of twinkling radiance.

"Good afternoon, Pat, fellows," Riley greeted them. "What is all this, then?"

Pat Kelly, his eyes looking unnaturally green, leaned on his shovel.

"We need you, Michael, so we came to collect you. I know you're not on duty till tomorrow, but Captain Fagan sent us to request all hands on deck."

Riley straightened. "I see."

"The city's at a standstill. News, goods, emergency services, and even firemen can't get through till the streets get cleared. It is a large task."

Riley gestured to Ben and Maj. "My tenants and I have just been saying that."

"I suggested this method of clearing the streets, and

Captain Fagan formed squads such as ours to visit officers' homes and call them on duty. Following that, we will recruit every automaton in the city to bring shovels and make up work crews."

Felicity had come down the walkway in time to hear the declaration.

"An automaton army," she proclaimed. "But one intended to fight only the snow."

Pat Kelly emitted the grinding sound that, for him, represented laughter. "Just so long as the coal holds out."

Riley turned to Ben and Maj. "Sir, miss, I must go. Will you hold the fort here?"

"Of course," Ben replied.

Riley faced Felicity. "Wife, you understand it is my duty to go."

"Yes. I do understand that."

Ben asked, "Officer Kelly, how long do you think it will take to clear the city?"

"Days, *sor*. We are filled with snow from east to west and north to south. The weather scholars are saying there has never been such a blizzard. 'Twas the wind that was the culprit, *sor*." He turned and waved an arm to the southwest. "Lake Erie being all frozen over, that wind came along, picked up all the snow left on the surface by previous storms, and dropped it square upon us."

Ben thought about it. "I'm sure the city can survive being shut down like this for a day or two. After that, people will need help. The elderly, the infirm." He thought of all the children in the orphanages scattered across the city. "They'll need food delivered and, as you say, coal."

Without coal, everything would grind to a halt. No light. No heat. No automatons.

What would Buffalo be without the automatons?

"That's why we're here, *sor*." Kelly said modestly. "We can work twenty-four hours a day without rest. Several of the crews will make directly for the coal warehouses."

"Yes, but such a task!" Ben's mind boggled.

Kelly told him almost gently, "This is our city too. Perhaps it is time we proved our investment in it."

Having collected Riley, they continued on to clear the rest of the street, taking with them stray automatons from the houses all around, including Gamet's wife, Maybell, who hurried out, puffing steam.

"If my Gamet remains too damaged to help," she declared, "I am strong enough to take his place."

Felicity stayed back at the Riley residence, and the three of them stood on the newly cleared front steps, watching the phenomenon chug back into action.

"I feel I should do something," Ben said. Like Maybell, he wanted to contribute.

Maj gazed at him in alarm. "I understand. It feels like an all-hands-on-deck moment. But why not wait till at least some of the main streets are cleared?"

"I suppose that would be wise. I hope Mother is doing all right, stranded with only Dora and that new unit she barely knows."

"You'll be able to check on her soon. Meanwhile, we'd better go inside and get warm."

From the top floor of the house, the sunlight having melted the glaze of ice from the windows so they could see out—street upon street unfolded with figures moving slowly, steadily along them. Crews formed of automatons.

They appeared small and ant-like against the

unending expanses of snow, drifted across block after block, chest high. Ben, standing and gazing out, could see them moving down Lafayette Avenue, the main thoroughfare closest to them. The sun winked on metal, both worn and shiny. From up here it was hard to tell them apart.

Still no vehicles moved anywhere, and aside from the scraping of shovels, voices calling across the distance, and the occasional bark of a dog, silence reigned.

They would never do it, Ben thought. Even metal working twenty-four hours a day could not accomplish such a herculean task.

He went to sleep that night after a small repast—they had to conserve their food—with Maj in his arms and the sound of distant shoveling in his ears.

Chapter Thirty-Three

Maj awoke to a profound and terrifying silence. She lay in the bed for a moment, her eyes stretched wide, and tried to decide why she felt so frightened.

Gray daylight trickled into the room. It must be very early. All around her lay—

Stillness.

The sound of shoveling had moved away so she could no longer hear it or, indeed, anything beyond the pounding of her own heart. The energy that always, on some level, flowed through her awareness remained hushed also, as if the city slept a sleep so deep it rivaled death.

And beyond that—

Nothing. She was alone.

She sat bolt upright in the bed and assessed her situation. Nobody except her in the bed—not even Pup. The door of the bedroom stood open. She could glimpse the other room and could see Pup standing there motionless, staring toward the door.

Ben.

He wasn't currently outside with Pup, because there the dog stood. Perhaps he'd risen to use the toilet. She felt the sheet beside her, fingers groping.

Cold.

No. Oh, no.

He wouldn't leave her. He wouldn't do anything so

foolish as to go out and shovel on his own, would he? Not without telling her, anyway.

Of course he knew very well if he told her she'd argue and she'd try and talk him out of it.

She leaped out of the bed and searched the set of rooms. It didn't take long, the place being so small. No Ben in the washroom or out in the hall. She stood and forced herself to calm enough she would be able to breathe.

"Pup? Where is he?"

Pup went to their outer door.

All right, then. Perhaps he'd gone down to the cellar to load the steam plant. Now that she thought about it, she couldn't hear the plant running, and the air in the house felt cold.

She'd start her search there.

Hastily she dressed and ran down, her feet clattering on the bare, wooden stairs. To reach the cellar she had to go through Felicity's flat—as, she realized, Ben would have also had to do.

She beat a tattoo on the door. No answer. She knocked again and had just decided to go out around the back when Felicity opened the door.

The automaton looked neat and tidy as usual. Maj didn't imagine she slept as such. However, something about her, maybe an air she emitted, told Maj that Felicity also felt on edge.

"Mrs. Riley, I'm sorry to bother you so early, but is Benjamin here? I woke up and—and I can't find him."

The words did not express the extent of the devastation that accompanied them.

"No, Miss Magenta, I am sorry. He is not here. In fact, I wish he were. I was just in the cellar examining the steam plant. It seems to have ceased running."

"Has it run out of coal?"

"No, that is not the problem. There is sufficient coal."

Maj tried to put her own troubles aside. "Would you like me to look at it?"

"That might be helpful." Felicity invited her in. "Do you know much about steam plants?"

Not as much as you, Maj thought, since in truth, Felicity was one beneath her hybrid skin. Most automatons in the city had to keep themselves running, unless a major failure that required repairs occurred.

She followed Felicity to the cellar where they both stood and looked at the furnace. Built of iron with a grated door, it usually glowed with heat and gave off a dim glow as it pounded out power to the rest of the house.

Now it lay silent. A mechanical problem? Or something more?

Maj closed her eyes for an instant, trying to sense what both Ben and Dirk had called the ley lines, the life force beneath the ground. If the energy beneath the city fell too low, would things like this steam plant die also?

No, that was foolishness. This was just a coincidence. A steam plant running nonstop in the cold might be expected to experience a failure.

She hauled open the door of the furnace and peered inside. "The fire's gone out. Maybe we just need to restart it."

"That was my own conclusion, and I have tried. As you might imagine, I am rather good at kindling a fire in a combustion chamber."

"Ah—yes."

"I have lit this one several times. The fire dwindles

and burns out just as if a breath has snuffed it."

"A reverse draft, perhaps. Maybe because it's so cold out, the chimney is not drawing."

"A fire usually draws best when there is a wide differentiation between indoor and outdoor temperatures."

"Uh—yes."

"I do not know what to do. The house will soon grow dangerously cold without the steam plant. The fire is the heart of the home."

A profound statement and one that might be applied to the city itself.

Maj snapped herself back to the moment. "Let's try lighting it again. Is the flue wide open?"

"It is."

Together they struggled. Not once, not twice, but thrice. Just as Felicity had said, the small flame snuffed out each time.

"I grow discouraged," Felicity said finally, which on the face of it seemed an incredible statement. "Michael is at work and I am charged with looking after his home. His home means much to him. I have failed."

The last words came in a wail.

"No, you haven't." Maj sought to reassure her. "You've done your very best."

Felicity waved her hands. "You do not understand. Units such as I are built to operate faultlessly. To be faultless. We must accomplish the tasks we are set. Our worth depends upon it."

Maj turned to face the hybrid. "That is not so. And you are much more than a unit."

"Am I?" Felicity's eyes were wide. "Beneath it all, I am just steel and steam."

"I do not think Michael married you for your ability to accomplish the tasks you are set. You did say he married you?"

"Yes. In the large ceremony at Delaware Park."

"Then it was because he cares for you." Who said metal was incapable of emotions? Loyalty, fear, love. Maj, herself exploring the degrees of love for the first time, saw that it could encompass need—for her and Ben, it certainly did. Michael and Felicity quite clearly also needed each other.

"Yes," Felicity said again. "But, Miss Magenta, deep within me is the requirement to be useful. You see, we were all created for that purpose and programmed accordingly, before anything else."

Everything, so Maj acknowledged, needed a purpose—even the city itself. Even Benjamin. So she'd had no right to try and coddle him. She could see that, but oh, it did nothing to curb the terror lurking inside her.

"Let's leave this for a while," she suggested. "The house will cool off slowly, and we still have the fires in the grates. Perhaps repairmen will be able to get through soon."

But she thought of all those packed white streets and the slowness of the progress clearing them.

Felicity nodded.

"You're certain you haven't seen Benjamin?"

"No, Miss Magenta. He did not come through my flat."

Then he must have gone out. There was no other possibility.

"Please, Felicity, return to your flat. I'll go upstairs also and make sure the fire is burning in my grate. Then I need to go out and search for Benjamin."

She ran back up with Pup at her heels and stood in the center of the parlor, staring around wildly.

How could he have gone without a word for her? He wouldn't. *He wouldn't.*

Carefully now, she began to search the rooms again. She found it on her second pass, a scrap of white paper that had fallen from the small table where they ate their meals and lay face down beneath it.

Gone to Mother's. Will see if I can get through. Back very soon. Don't worry.

Maj gave a hollow laugh.

Don't worry? He might as well say, "Don't breathe." He was her heartbeat. Her very life.

And he was out there. Somewhere. In this big, frozen city that was dying by degrees.

Chapter Thirty-Four

She bundled up in layers and debated over leaving Pup at home. In the end she decided to take him, thinking he might be of some use in snuffling Ben out, though once she got outside it became quite evident all he would smell was snow.

Snow City, indeed. The national newspapers got it right. Today, unlike yesterday, the sun did not shine quite so bright. Instead, a milky stew of clouds streamed in from over the lake. More snow coming? Please, no.

Their street had been cleared but she didn't know how many others had, or what main arteries had been hooked up. Standing down here in her boots felt quite different from her perch up at the top of the house where she could see for blocks and blocks.

Which route would Ben have taken? His house lay on Virginia Street and her most direct route would be Delaware Avenue, one of the main arteries of the city. She recalled from the book Ben had brought her that, indeed, Delaware ran directly over one of the ley lines that threaded the area.

She set out in that direction with Pup scampering after. Many of the homes had been at least partially cleared of snow. Some lay still drifted in, and silent. No one home, perhaps, or no automatons in the household. They looked odd with only their upper stories protruding from the pristine white mounds.

It took her half a block to realize the truth. Buffalo, usually a bustling city that ran on steam, customarily smelled of coal smoke. It still did, but the tang was surprisingly faint. The air had been swept clean by the wind, and yet—

Her eyes told her the truth. Skipping her gaze from house to house, she located each chimney.

A mere fraction of them emitted any smoke.

Her heart gave a sickening lurch when she grasped what that must mean: Riley's house wasn't the only one wherein the steam plant had shut down. Indeed, a number of those on Lafayette Avenue, which she'd reached, appeared cold.

Why was this? And what might the ramifications be? Some of these homes, those where the snow had not been shoveled, could indeed stand empty, their occupants caught away by the storm, stranded elsewhere. But eyeing the chimneys she saw some of those that had been shoveled out also remained smokeless.

At one or two, she noticed occupants outside still shoveling. On impulse, Maj approached one of them.

The individual proved to be a large and battered steam unit who worked steadily removing the snow from a front pathway, lifting it high onto a heap that filled the lawn. When Maj reached him, he paused in his work and regarded her with worn, painted eyes.

"Miss? Can I help?"

"Perhaps. We live over on Congress Street, and our steam plant's gone out. I notice there's no smoke coming from your chimney either. Are you also having problems?"

"Yes, miss. My fellow worker has been endeavoring all night to keep it alight. An impossible task, as it has proven. Our employer is very cold."

"I notice many of the other houses on the street are failing to emit any smoke." Maj stared into the painted face. "Something is very wrong."

"Yes, miss."

"I wonder how far the problem reaches, across the city."

"I do not know, miss. I have been nowhere else."

A simple unit without much imagination, he did not seem particularly troubled. Yet things were not always what they seemed.

He added, "My employer, Miss Beck, wishes to call a repairman, but none can get through. I am clearing the way."

A practical attempt to remedy the situation, to be sure. Yet panic licked at Maj. A veritable troop of repairmen couldn't fix this.

She said to the unit, just to have the words out in the air, "The city has ground to a halt."

"Yes, miss."

Could anyone save it?

With Pup still at her heels, she left the steam unit and went on to Delaware. There, her ears once more caught the sound of many shovels being employed.

Delaware Avenue had, after a fashion, been cleared. Normally a broad thoroughfare, it now consisted of a track less than half its normal width, yet it did allow for traffic. Indeed, here she saw her first vehicle, an ambulance struggling to progress southward.

As she'd already discovered, ice underlay the snow. The tires on the vehicle—one of the new steam ambulances—slid and shuddered. A number of automatons, including several hybrids, helped push it along.

Maj ran forward and lent her own strength. The ambulance successfully pulled away, and she turned to look at her neighbor.

He was a tall hybrid, well-bundled, with fair hair and eyes so blue they were startling. He appeared cheerful, unbothered by what was taking place all around him, and gave her a smile even as she did a double take.

"Thank you for the help, miss."

"I know you." Her mind put it together. "You're the captain of the Steamers Hockey Team."

"Nils Nilsson, miss, at your service." He gave her a second sunny smile. "Nice doggie." He spoke with an accent. "What is his name?"

"Er—Pup."

"That is a very apt name."

"Yes, I suppose it is. Do you know how much of Delaware Avenue has been cleared?"

"The crews are still working their way southward. It is slow work."

"I understand." If the street hadn't been cleared all the way to Virginia, Ben wouldn't be able to reach his mother's house. Where would he go then? Might she meet him on the way back?

Nilsson gestured to his companions. "The team and I decided to make ourselves useful, since useful is a very good thing to be. We are pushing out vehicles wherever they get stuck. There are many." He cocked his head slightly at Maj. "Do you need assistance?"

No. Yes. What might this strapping automaton do for her?

"I'm looking for someone. Perhaps you saw him come this way." She spouted out a description of Ben that included the color of his coat.

"I notice much, me. I am programmed to collect details and coordinate them. I regret to say I did not see this man you describe."

Maj's heart fell. "I'll continue searching then. Thank you anyway."

"Miss—?"

"Magenta. It's Magenta Rask."

"The team and I are moving about all these streets seeking to help. If we see this man I will tell him Magenta Rask is looking for him."

"Yes. His name is Benjamin Ambrose, and he is— he is vital to the welfare of this city."

Nils Nilsson's expression turned serious. "Then if found, we will take very good care of him. I have never seen the city so quiet. I do not like it."

"Neither do I."

He gestured again to his team, who stood by in a group, following their exchange. "Would you like one of us to accompany you?"

"That's not necessary. I think he's heading for Virginia Street and I don't know how far he'll get. You keep doing your good work."

His smile flashed again. "You may be sure we will!" He hesitated before he added, "Because this is our city too."

Yes. Yes it was.

Maj thought about it as she turned up the half-tunnel that was Delaware Avenue. The city belonged equally to all of them. If it died, they would all lose.

If they could somehow keep it alive, they would all win. Together.

Only if they saw and recognized that truth would they survive.

Chapter Thirty-Five

Ben made excruciatingly slow progress on his way to Virginia Street and decided almost immediately it had been a very poor idea to try. Sneaking out on Magenta while she still slept had been unfair. So had not telling her honestly what he meant to do.

He had not wanted to worry her—she fretted for him so—or to begin another lengthy recitation on her part of all the reasons he should not go. He knew very well why he should not go. But he felt a moral obligation toward his mother.

Now that he was out here on the streets, though, it felt wrong. The whole city felt wrong. He might not usually, consciously, be able to feel the energy trails below the ground the way Magenta could. Yet according to her, they were somehow connected to him, or rather he fed off them. If they flagged, so did he.

Not a reassuring thought, and he almost turned back when it came to him. Guilt and obligation, however, rode him hard. He'd abandoned Mother, left her on her own with only Dora and a stranger of a steam unit. It wasn't so very many blocks to Virginia Street, at least not on your average day. He could make sure Mother and the household were all right and hopefully pop back home before Magenta woke up.

However, he didn't make it as far as Virginia Street. Instead he ran into the back of an automaton work crew similar to the one that had cleared Congress.

He'd seen a couple other such crews on the side streets he passed, working steadily and shedding snow to either side like a giant machine.

Well, they were machines, though made up of components that varied almost comically. He could not guess from whence the various steam units had come, whether their owners and employers had sent them out or they were independent, like Riley and Gamet. Some were large, some barely as high as Ben's shoulder. Some were old and battered, some new and shining. They worked together with one unwavering, single-minded purpose.

He followed them south down Delaware Avenue in a slow progress, wishing he had a shovel and could help. A cold wind snaked up out of the southwest and struck him in the face. He pictured the big lake stretching all the way back into Ohio, its black ice winking, its breath enough to freeze the blood.

When his fingers and toes began to tingle, he didn't think much of it. His boots and gloves were losing the battle against the cold air, that was all. Not till his heart began beating double-time up in his chest and the world around him began to waver did he panic.

No, oh no. Not this. Not now. He could not die out here in the street with no one able to save him close at hand.

Oh, God. *Magenta*. He had left her. She would never forgive him.

He reached Allen Street, which looked partially cleared, and turned up it. The progress of the automatons was too slow. He'd never reach home that way, not before he gave in to what beset him and collapsed. He was scarcely a block from Mother's house. Some of the side streets near the corner looked clear. If he could find a way through a yard—

But he was already starting to lose sensation and his connection with the world. Too late, too late to turn back or call to the army of automatons for help. Sheer willpower took him up a narrow street, only partially cleared, that he thought should reach through to Virginia Steet. It didn't, and by the time he came up against the wall of pure snow at which it ended, he could barely see for the dots before his eyes. Even the sound of his own footsteps escaped his ears.

Magenta, he thought as he fell, as the cold of the snow came up and met him, pounded through him. As he melted into the city and became part of it.

The way he'd always and forever been.

****

Frustration fogged all Magenta's senses, clogged her throat, and pooled in her stomach. Not two blocks from Virginia Street, where Ben's house lay, she'd come upon the rear of a work crew, one like that which had come down Congress Street and those she'd spied elsewhere along the way.

Worse, much worse than that, she hadn't found Benjamin.

He must have come this way. His note had said so. And besides Delaware Avenue, there were no viable alternative routes.

So why hadn't she caught up with him? He should have been cooling his heels at the rear of this crew just like her. She should have had her hands on him by now, easing this terrible yawning ache inside.

She had to catch him before the city finished dying.

Despite the work crews, despite the life that slowly trailed back in the form of the ambulance and a couple of horse-drawn drays, it was well on its way to death. More and more buildings she passed lay cold and dark—everything from homes to businesses to factories whose chimneys she'd never before seen idle.

She closed her eyes and tried to sense what was happening underground. Very little. Like a spring in the thick of winter, the energy had very nearly frozen and stopped flowing.

She stamped her foot in frustration. She had to get through!

Pup gave a bark.

"Excuse me, excuse me, I have to get through." Pushing at shovels right and left, very nearly getting beaned in the head, she battered a path through the work crew that blocked the way in front of her. She couldn't tell who was leading this particular group. The first row, all standard automatons, worked in unison. Making her way with difficulty to the front, she flattened herself against the wall of snow at which they aimed, with Pup barking furiously.

One of the two center units, a large and powerful automaton, froze with his shovel aloft and said to her, "Please move, miss. You are putting yourself in danger. And your little dog too."

"I don't care. I need your help." If she understood automatons correctly, they would have a strong desire to assist her and could not resist such a direct appeal.

This towering unit could not blink at her or otherwise display surprise, but he recoiled slightly and lowered his shovel.

"Help how? We are already helping. We have a job

to do."

"Yes, I understand. Your crew is marvelous. But I have to get down there." She pointed vaguely at the wall of snow in the direction of Virginia Street. "It's terribly important."

"We have instructions to clear Delaware Avenue. It is an important thoroughfare."

"You're right, it is. One of the main arteries of the city. But—" Desperate, she reached out and touched his metal skin, seeking a connection. "I have to find someone, and I think he's gone down there."

"Is he in one of those houses? If so, you will have to wait for the secondary streets to be cleared."

"I know."

"I warn you, it may take days. I am informed automatons are out all over the city forming an army to clear snow. However, there are many, many streets."

"I understand that, but I can't wait. Please. I can't explain it and I know it doesn't make sense, but this person for whom I'm searching is vitally important to the city."

The unit turned its head and looked at each of his flanking units, in turn.

The one on his left said, "I do not think we should deviate from our assignment."

"Yet," said the one on the right, "the young lady seems most vehement."

"Vehement! Yes, I am vehement. Please. It is not many houses down."

"We will take a vote on it. This is a democratic society." The first unit turned around to face the crew.

"This young woman wishes us to veer our course and clear a way through to Virginia Street. She says it is vitally important. Those of you who believe we should carry on with our assigned task, raise your shovels."

A forest of shovels went up. These were simple units, created to follow instructions and complete their assignments. But they were also a generation of automatons allowed for the first time to make their own decisions.

Maj cried out to them, "Those of you who want to save our city, raise your shovels!"

Nearly every shovel went up, which Maj figured meant several units had voted twice.

She didn't care.

The work crew turned toward Virginia Street.

Chapter Thirty-Six

As above, so below.

The words shivered through Benjamin in a faint reverberation. He could not say they echoed in his ears because he no longer appeared to have ears.

Or a corporal form.

Indeed, his body seemed to be laid beneath him as he viewed it from the air. At first, he took the form lying in the snow of the alleyway for a crumpled pile of clothing. Familiar clothing. The coat, made of dark blue wool, was his coat. Same with the hat and gloves. His.

He floated in the air between two houses at the height of the second story, looking down at himself.

This could not be good.

He'd tried to hold on, but the sensation had overtaken him as he ran. Tingling in the extremities. The pounding of the heart, madly rapid as that tingling climbed through his body. A buzzing in the head. He must have fallen. Was he dead? He'd never gotten to this point before in the process of dying. Always someone had been there to intervene.

Now he lay alone. No one knew where he was, on some side street little more than an alleyway between two houses. If he wasn't already dead, the cold would soon finish him.

But he must be already dead. Why else would he be floating here and not back inside his body?

As above, so below. As within, so without.

The words sounded like the tolling of a distant bell. He wanted to know what they meant. Then again, he did not want to abandon his body, lying there like a broken hybrid automaton.

He rose higher into the air, past the second story windows of the house beside him, past the eaves and the roof so drifted with snow it looked like a lopsided hat. He saw—

Oh, from up here he could see everything. The city spread out before him, block upon block, street after street, most still filled with snow. He could see the pattern of it all, the beauty with which it had been laid out, and the land beyond, undulating to hills far in the south.

He could see the river to his right, rushing, with chunks of ice hurtling along, bobbing against each other and the shore.

He could see the vast lake.

If he'd had a body that could draw breath, he would have sucked in a great gust, in awe. The lake stretched dark, frozen over, its long, black surface cleared by the wind, all the snow dumped on the city. Ben had never before seen it from up this high or dreamed of doing so. It looked both frightening and magnificent, like a sleeping beast.

As above, so below.

What did that mean?

From up here all the houses looked more or less the same. You couldn't tell which were owned by humans and which by automatons. Likewise the churches. He could see the spires here and there, reaching up like fingers pointing to a proposed heaven. But he couldn't say which had been raised by flesh and which by steam.

Most of the chimneys, as he could see from up here—and there were many—emitted no smoke and looked cold.

The city was dying. Why? It was dying above because below—

The energy that flowed, the streams called ley lines that somehow fed and sustained this place, had stilled and frozen, choked by conflict, by discord. By hate. Maj had been right all along. That which kept the city alive kept him alive also.

Only he was no longer alive. And he did not want to float here watching the city he loved die.

Maj. Oh, what would she do without him? They'd only just found each other, yet the loss bit deep. Deep. And Mother—he'd had no chance to say goodbye.

Regret tugged at him even as he drifted higher like a smut of soot lifting before being blown away. The heap that was his body grew more distant, as did the energy that lay beneath the streets, beneath the mighty river, and the lake itself.

The wind caught him and drew him aloft. He did not see a door open from one of the houses onto the alleyway or the small, battered steamie that trundled out. A humble unit, the lowest of the low in this city, of barely any worth. Yet it noticed the bundle of castoff clothing with its unseeing eyes, and moved its squeaking wheels toward it, carrying a small fire for a heart.

****

Desperation hammered in Maj's skull, so hard she felt she might perish from the inside out. It clamored in time with the shovels and with her wild heartbeat.

A part of her searched everywhere for a familiar

form—the blue woolen coat. The brown hair and deceptively ordinary face.

Benjamin Ambrose, anything but ordinary, went about like a modest, unexceptional man, not recognizing his own worth.

But his absence—that would be felt.

Ever since the riot in Niagara Square a year and a half ago, the city had been in turmoil, hate and discord on the rise. Last summer's plague had worsened things because it had weakened the city by damaging its heart.

As she'd come to understand, it was all about the heart. The energy that ran below the surface, the city's bloodstream. Acts of goodness, of kindness, so she believed, kept the city alive.

Now hate combined with the paralyzing effects of the blizzard had it very nearly ground to a halt.

But where was Benjamin? Surely, surely she had followed his path, the only one he could have taken. He could not have disappeared between home and Virginia Street.

Yet they'd very nearly reached his mother's house, the wide phalanx of automatons working steadily and she following behind. One or two of them had dropped out to go in search of coal, but the rest worked on, cutting an inexorable path through the cloaking snow.

When they reached it, Ben's house looked cold and dark. No smoke came from the chimney. Next door, at a red brick house, the entire household appeared to be outside clearing snow. A man with an ancient steamie and a squadron of children all paused in their work as Maj ran up the front steps of the Ambrose house, which someone had cleared, after a fashion.

She'd reached her goal but had little real hope in her

heart of finding Ben here. How could he have reached this place ahead of her with that wall of snow blocking the street?

Nevertheless, she pounded on the door in time with her beating heart. The automaton called Dora answered and stared at her, and at Pup by her feet.

"Is Ben here?" Maj demanded. "Benjamin Ambrose. Is he—?"

"Miss Rask?" Ben's mother appeared behind the automaton. She looked terrible, her face white and pinched, and she wore her coat over her dress. "What is it? Is it Ben? I could feel—"

"He's not here?" Maj's heart fell still farther, past her feet and into the stone threshold. "I've lost him, Mrs. Ambrose. I've lost him!" It came out in a wail.

"Come in." After a look at all the staring faces next door, Mrs. Ambrose drew Maj into the entry, which felt cold and lay steeped in gloom. The woman didn't even seem to notice the dog that trotted into her foyer, making a trail of snow.

"I woke up this morning and he was gone. He left me a note saying he meant to check on you. To come here. But the streets are mostly all blocked. He couldn't get here, could he, before they cleared the street?"

"Oh, God." Mrs. Ambrose twisted her hands together. "Oh, God."

"Where could he be? Surely somewhere between here and the house on Congress." Could she have missed him along the way? But she'd looked for him. She'd *felt* for him.

"I was afraid of this." Mrs. Ambrose trembled where she stood. "I feared if he left this place where he was kept safe, I would never see him again."

245

"Mister Benjamin," wailed the automaton maid, who stood by. "Is he dead?"

Maj's eyes met Mrs. Ambrose's.

"Do not hate me," Maj begged. "I wanted, more than you can know, to keep him safe. Anyway, I believe hate is what's killing the city. And him."

"Find him. Find him, girl, and I'll give him to you gladly. I care not what or who you are."

A small measure of accord. Beneath the stone tiles of the entry, beneath the foundation and the earth below it, and the rock still farther down, Meg felt a trickle of energy release.

Would it be enough? Could she follow that trickle?

She must, if it wasn't too late.

Chapter Thirty-Seven

Maj stood in the middle of the intersection at Virginia and Delaware and closed her eyes. Sensing. *Sensing.*

Seldom before had she striven to deliberately use the latent power within her, that which Topaz Gideon assured her she possessed. For most of her life, she'd half feared it. It had been one of the many things that made her different, made her *other*. In her world, "different" was a hard thing to be.

Wasn't it enough that she was homeless, motherless, and without other family? Cast upon a population of the city that kept itself fed by nefarious means. Knowing nothing of herself except what she could see—that she was small, and probably of mixed blood—and what she could feel—the life force that streamed through others and beneath this city she loved.

Except now. Now, amid the hate that divided flesh and metal, and the frozen block imposed by the blizzard, it had nearly ceased to flow.

She felt the absence of that life force the way she would miss her own heartbeat. Her own, or his.

She searched for him. Standing there with the snowbound streets stretching around her and the clouds streaming overhead, she called upon abilities that had accompanied her always and that she had determinedly refused to acknowledge.

And found nothing.

She wanted to weep. She wanted to wail and stamp her feet. None of those actions would get her anywhere.

An automaton had followed her out from Benjamin's house. Not the little maid. This was an aged and scrappy unit, and must be the one Pike's Repair had sent to fill in for Winston.

She turned to him. Just a single woman and a single steamie to save Ben. To save the city.

"Help me," she cried.

"Miss, that is my reason."

"Your reason?"

"For being built. For existing. What shall I do?"

"Ask. Ask everyone. He's a tall man with brown hair, wearing a dark blue coat. He must have come this way. You take that side. I'll take this. Knock on doors. Ask."

The unit trundled off. Maj, still searching frantically for that trickle of energy deep underground, followed her own instructions.

With the street at least partially cleared, folks had started to emerge from the houses and businesses along the way. Steam units began to clear walkways, and humans surveyed the weather as if they might predict what it would do next.

With Pup now clutched in her arms Maj approached all of them, flesh and metal alike, and inquired after Ben. She stopped a man on a horse and an automaton digging a steamcab from a mound of snow at the curb. She approached a tradesman trying to decide whether to open his business and got the same response:

"I have not seen him."

No, she wanted to say, but have you felt him? Steady

and warm, solid as bedrock except for that devastating crack that runs through him. He's nearly the direct opposite of me. But together we—together—

Her thoughts stuttered there. Would they ever be together again?

She moved her way back down the main thoroughfare with despair growing in her heart. She could feel her own energy draining away and wondered what would happen to her if—

If Ben was gone.

No matter. With Ben gone, she wouldn't want to live.

"Miss? Miss!"

The call, which was mechanical in nature, came from the far side of the street and snagged her attention. The ancient unit from Ben's house stood there waving his arms at her.

"Over here!"

Her heart leaped. The unit stood at the intersection of a lane that had been only partially cleared alongside a second unit, very small and battered, puffing visible steam. Maj set Pup down and raced across to them.

"Miss, I believe he is here in this alley."

The small unit ground out a stream of words from a scratchy voice box. "You are looking for human in blue coat. But I think this one is dead."

No. Maj stumbled and drew herself up by sheer force of will. "Show me."

They battled their way up the alleyway, in truth no more than a space meant for trash cans, supposed to cut through to Virginia Street but blocked on the end by the seemingly inevitable wall of snow.

Beside the wall of snow lay a figure in a dark blue

coat, sprawled on his back, both arms outflung.

"I did turn him over," the tiny unit said. "To see if he was alive. He is not breathing."

With a gasp, Maj threw herself down in the snow beside Benjamin. She didn't notice the cold that penetrated her skirt and stung her knees. She barely noticed the two units hovering nearby or the fact that little Pup snuggled in close to Ben, at her side.

"Ben? Ben!" She touched his face. Still, so still. Cold even to her chilled fingers. It might have been carved from ice.

His glasses had fallen off. His chocolate-brown eyes, wide open, stared sightlessly. Not at her but at the sky. No breath lifted his chest.

She unbuttoned his coat anyway and laid her ear there, against his body. She already knew the rhythm of his heart, had slept through the night while listening to it.

Silent now.

Emotions erupted inside her. A great well of pain. And protest. And, most of all, terror.

How could she go on without him? How could she continue breathing, if he did not? Of all the devastating occurrences in her life, this—

Was the worst.

"Miss," said the small unit, "I think he is dead."

"No." She said it aloud this time. "No!"

She curled her fingers into fists which she planted against Ben's chest. She narrowed her eyes, screwed up her face and her will, and reached deep inside.

It would not end here in this half-clogged alley, not for him or for her. Or for Snow City.

Chapter Thirty-Eight

If Maj had never before this day attempted to summon the power that lay within her, neither had she ever tried to wield it. She'd accepted that it accompanied her through her days, only sometimes rearing its head and claiming her attention.

Topaz insisted she could make it serve her, if she dared. If she embarked on a kind of apprenticeship and learned how. She'd had no interest in anything resembling schooling.

Now—now that it meant so much, she didn't know how to make the power answer her will. She had only crude supposition and raw desire to tell her how to proceed. And as she could clearly feel, the energies were low.

Yet she was above all else a heedless woman. And she was willing to expand all she had, all she was, to bring this man back.

So she disregarded the snow and the houses hemming her in on either side, the distressed dog and the two automatons that watched her.

She reached deep.

Streams tend to freeze up in the winter. Even a city girl knew that. The Niagara abounded with chunks of ice. And Lake Erie lay surfaced with it.

A winter of both season and spirit had seized Buffalo. Hatred and discord. Distrust and an insistence on differences. The life that usually flowed so generously beneath this place had locked down tight.

But the city was stronger than that. It had been born of differences coming together, of those who had come from elsewhere. From the south where they had been formerly held in chains. From overseas where they had been ostracized, belittled, and shunned. From foundries and metal shops. From graveyards.

All these things met. All these things came together to make something else, something more. Something that could exist nowhere else on earth.

Beneath Maj's knees, beneath the snow and the brick and the rock, she felt the energy—faint as it was—stir. A mere thread it had become, trickling through the frozen blockade of hate. But she focused on it. Latched onto it. Exerted all her will and *pulled*.

The energy responded to her, but only sluggishly. She too felt depleted. As she'd learned while with Ben, though, like called to like even when divided by distance. The power running through the ley lines wanted to come to her. It *wanted* to return.

Come then, she called to it. She set her knees and raised her clenched fists and groaned at the sky. *Come!*

Beneath its burden of ice, the river trembled. A tremor passed down the length of the frozen lake. And beneath the bedrock the power leaped up. It rose in a wild, crazy surge, and the lifeblood of the city began once more to flow.

From east to west, from north to south, it cracked the paralysis that held it. At that instant Maj—Maj was its heart.

For this moment of time, her will pounded through it, set the beat, drove the rising blood. That blood warmed and further diminished the ice that held it. The city strained against the darkness and leaped to life.

Feeling that, Maj wanted to weep but couldn't spare the attention for it. Perhaps tears did trickle down her face, but she disregarded them. Joy possessed her, fierce and illuminating joy enough to burn her up.

When it reached its peak, when it filled her to overflowing, she lowered her fists—which still figuratively grasped the energy—and laid them against Benjamin's chest.

His heart jerked to life.

It did not take much. So great was the power that filled Maj, the merest touch enlivened him and started the blood flowing in his veins just the way the energy flowed beneath the earth.

There in the humblest alley, witnessed by only herself and the two aged automatons, the miracle occurred.

Sound came with it. Voices called from several streets over, doors banged. A rumbling from the homes on either side—first one and then the other—told her their steam plants had come to life. Pup gave a happy bark.

Ben's eyes, still open, filled with awareness. He blinked a few times before he found her face and drew a deep breath.

"Maj?"

Only then did she crumble. She collapsed onto his chest, her fists now clutching the front of his coat, and wept.

"Here now," he murmured. "Can you help me up?"

It was not easy, with Pup frolicking and trying to crawl into his lap. She managed with help from one of the steam units. Ben visibly took stock of himself, examined both of his hands, and patted down his chest before he looked at Maj again.

"I think I was dead."

"Yes."

"I remember—I was trying to cut through to Virginia Street. To reach Mother. And I felt it begin. I must have gone down right here."

"It's all right. I found you." She picked his specs up from the snow and placed them very gently on his face. "I found you and it will never happen again."

"I'm—"

"Cured," she assured him. "And so is the city, I think."

"How?"

"It's love," she told him. "The cure for anything is love."

****

They helped him out of the alley, around the corner, and onto Virginia Street since he insisted on walking. With Maj on one side of him and Roland on the other, they went slowly but steadily, dodging pedestrians who stared and a couple of steamcabs already out on the street.

When they reached his mother's house, a number of people outside at the McMahons' came running. One of them proved to be Liam McMahon.

"Ambrose? By God, man! Don't tell me it happened again?"

"Yes."

"Are ye after needin' my wife's help? She's just inside."

"Thanks, but no. As you can see, I'm up and

moving. Thanks to Maj, here."

A wise look came into the Irishman's blue eyes. "A good woman is all any man truly needs."

Ben's mother came running out of the house. "Oh! Oh, my goodness. Let us get him inside!"

They did, with Ben still leaning on Maj and the steamie rattling behind.

"What happened?" Ben's mother demanded. "Did you—"

"I died, Mother. I died and was very nearly gone for good. Maj called me back again."

His mother turned to Maj and pulled her into a fierce embrace. "Thank you, my girl. You are welcome, most welcome to my home."

Maj withdrew from the embrace far enough to look Ben's mother in the eye. "And your son? Am I also welcome to him?"

"Him," Mother declared, "I suspect you have already claimed as your own."

Chapter Thirty-Nine

"Look what it says here." Maj crawled into the big bed with the news sheet and shook it open across Ben's lap.

She must have picked it up when she took Pup out for his morning piddle. Since only three days had passed since Ben had been dead, she'd insisted he stay here in the warm bed.

He didn't mind. A part of him enjoyed the pampering he'd received since they came home from his mother's house. Besides, he figured if he stayed put long enough, she'd make love to him. Again.

"What is it?" he asked indulgently. Pup jumped up on the bed and Ben fed him the crust of his toast. Crumbs be damned.

He snaked an arm around Maj and cuddled her close.

"They're holding a special election. In three days." She settled more comfortably. "Read it to me."

He did. " 'Special election to be held for the office of mayor.' It looks like the post will start out temporary and become permanent at the end of what would have been Mayor Piffin's term."

Mayor Piffin, as had been discovered when his house in the old First Ward got shoveled out, had failed to survive the blizzard despite the fact that he'd followed his own advice for doing so. When found in his home, he lay surrounded by empty Buffalo's Best Beer bottles. His home had been one in which the steam plant had gone out. It had not restarted after Maj summoned up the ley lines, which had likely been too late for him anyway. Apparently the good mayor, in a stupor, had frozen to death.

Most other homes in the city, though, had revived. Just like Ben himself.

He had no doubt he owed that to Maj. He'd half felt the way she'd summoned him, along with the power that brought—and now kept—him alive.

She'd cured him. And the city. Why, the articles filling the news sheet proved it. Except for the story about Mayor Piffin, they were all positive things. Stories about the human and metal components of the city working together. Of help being offered on every hand. Why, here was a headline about a ceremony of thanks, spawned by the formerly militant Boilermakers' Union, to the armies of automatons that had cleared the streets.

It had taken two days. And nights. Every operable automaton in Buffalo had gone out to the task and had reclaimed the city, brought it back to sound and motion. For the benefit of all.

The energy beneath the streets now flowed strong once more. Maj had assured Ben of that, though she hadn't really needed to tell him. He could feel it flowing through his own veins. And through her, when they made love. He'd never felt so well.

Maj brought his attention back to the lead story. "See who the candidates for mayor are? Three of them."

"Conrad Fink. He's the head of the Automaton Expulsion League, isn't he? Or was."

Mr. Fink had changed his tune since the storm, had

stopped talking the automatons down, and even said the city owed a great debt to them.

"And Theodore Collwys. He's a lawyer and takes on a lot of cases on behalf of the disadvantaged, including automatons. He's married to Georgina, who's a good friend of Mrs. McMahon, next door to Mother."

Maj tucked her head onto Ben's shoulder. "I like Mrs. McMahon."

"So do I."

She tapped the newssheet with one finger. "And the third candidate?"

Ben read and blinked. "Patrick Kelly? But he's—"

"A hybrid automaton." Maj slewed around in the bed and seized the front of Ben's sleep shirt. "Oh, Ben, do you think it's possible he could be elected?"

"I don't know. Do you?"

"I hope so. I really do. He's so sensible and well-spoken. And well-liked even by those who don't normally favor hybrids."

"He has a sketchy past, though. He was created by those madmen, Mason and Charles. Created to be a killer."

"That was a long time ago. Now he's the head of the Irish Squad, with a human wife and a little girl. He's a blend of everything this city contains. I think he'd make a splendid mayor."

"If you think it," Ben planted a kiss on her lips, "it will be so."

She stared at him out of black eyes lit by a spark of—well, he didn't even have words to describe what that was.

"Meaning—" She made the word a tease.

"Meaning if you set your mind to something in this

city, Miss Magenta Rask, it most likely will happen. You have your finger on the pulse of Buffalo, after all."

"It's a good city. A wonderful city, full of potential. Full of second chances. Everybody has come here for that—a second chance. And they're all doing such good in their own ways. I want them all to succeed."

"Then they will."

"But look here—the national papers are still calling us Snow City. Do you think we'll ever live down that reputation?"

"Probably not."

"That's a shame. We're so much more than our weather. They should call us Strong City. Or Kind City. Or Generous City."

"Maybe," Ben suggested, "Buffalo should just be called the City of Good Neighbors. All right, bright, and healed. Why don't you kiss me, magical Magenta Rask? And then marry me. Together, we will make it so."

A word about the author…

Born in Buffalo and raised on the Niagara Frontier, Laura Strickland has been an avid reader and writer since childhood.

To her the spunky, tenacious, undefeatable ethnic mix that is Buffalo spells the perfect setting for a little Steampunk, so she created her own Victorian world there. She knows the people of Buffalo are stronger, tougher and smarter than those who haven't survived the muggy summers and blizzard blasts found on the shores of the mighty Niagara. Tough enough to survive a squad of automatons? Well, just maybe.